BBC

DOCTOR WHO

THE COMPANION'S COMPANION

By CLARA OSWALD

BBC CHILDREN'S BOOKS
UK | USA | Canada | Ireland | Australia | India | New Zealand | South Africa

BBC Children's Books are published by Puffin Books, part of the Penguin Random House group of companies whose addresses can be found at global.penguinrandomhouse.com.

www.penguin.co.uk www.puffin.co.uk www.ladybird.co.uk

Penguin Random House UK

First published 2017
001

Written by Craig Donaghy
Illustrations by Dan Green

Printed in China
A CIP catalogue record for this book is available from the British Library
ISBN: 978–1–405–92969–1

Well done on finding this book. I hid it in the one place in the TARDIS that I knew the Doctor would never look – but you would.

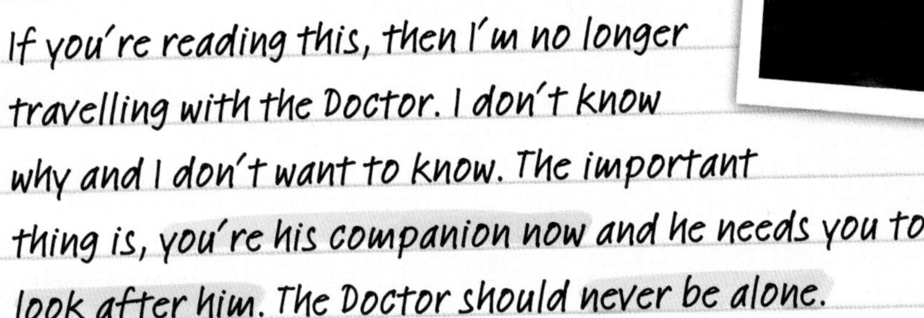

If you're reading this, then I'm no longer travelling with the Doctor. I don't know why and I don't want to know. The important thing is, you're his companion now and he needs you to look after him. The Doctor should never be alone.

As I've travelled through time and space I've been secretly putting together this guide just for you. I've gathered stories about and artefacts from his old companions, so you've got everything you need to be the best companion ever – so you can help the Doctor.

One thing is for sure: your life will never be the same again. So always be brave . . . and always be ready to run!

Clara Oswald

x

CONTENTS

TELL THEM NO GUNS. THE DOCTOR DOESN'T LIKE GUNS!

THERE'S A LOT TO TAKE IN!

6 Who is the Doctor?
8 Different Doctors
10 The Twelfth Doctor
14 Face Facts
18 First Things First!

YES, I'M AWARE THAT THIS DOESN'T COME FIRST!

20 A History of Companions
32 All About Aliens: Daleks
34 Donna's Diary
40 TARDIS Travel Essentials: Part One
42 How to Solve a Mystery in Five Steps!
44 All About Aliens: Silents
46 How to Pretend You Don't Travel in Time and Space
47 How to Admit You Travel in Time and Space
48 Pond Mail
50 Sonic Shades and Screwdrivers
52 Care Cards

THE DOCTOR WILL NEED THESE.

56 Travel in the TARDIS
60 UNIT Report: The Doctor, by Martha Jones
62 Lots of Doctors!
64 Most Wanted: Part One
66 Who Can Help? Part One: UNIT
68 All About Aliens: Dream Crabs
70 Rose Tyler's Emails
72 Conversations with the Doctor
77 Top Ten Reasons Why the Doctor Shouldn't Travel Alone VERY IMPORTANT!
78 Not the Doctor!
82 Letter from Grace Holloway
84 All About Aliens: Zygons
86 TARDIS Travel Essentials: Part Two
88 The Paternoster Gang's Rules

THESE GUYS KNOW THEIR STUFF!

90 Ace Notes
92 Most Wanted: Part Two
94 Monster Watch!
96 Which Companion Are You Most Like?
98 What's Your Sonic?
100 Rory's Weirdest Moments

THIS GUY IS HILARIOUS!

102 Postcards from Peri
104 Time with K-9 AFFIRMATIVE!

106 Keep the Doctor Away From . . .
108 All About Aliens: Ice Warriors
110 Yes or No!
112 Who Can Help? Part Two: Dorium Maldovar and Captain Jack
114 Friends and Family
116 All the Doctors!
118 How to Win!
120 How to Hunt Ghosts!
122 All About Aliens: Weeping Angels
124 Life After the Doctor
126 The Name of the Doctor
127 A Note from Strax
128 An Interview with Tegan
130 Alien First Aid
132 The Fourth Doctor, by Sarah Jane Smith
134 TARDIS Travel Essentials: Part Three
136 How to be Brave
138 All About Aliens: The Master, AKA Missy
140 Where Are They Now?
146 UNIT Report: The Doctor, by Josephine Grant
148 My Guide to the Doctors, by River Song
152 Who Can Help? Part Three: Craig Owens and Brian Williams
154 Jamie McCrimmon's Adventures with the Second Doctor
156 All About Aliens: Cybermen
158 Who Can Help? Part Four: Missy and Ashildr
160 A Letter from Susan Foreman
162 TARDIS Travel Essentials: Part Four
164 All About Aliens: Silurians
166 How to Manage the Doctor
168 Clara's Companion Quiz
174 Companion Certificate

HAVE I MENTIONED I'VE MET ALL THE DOCTORS? WELL, SORT OF.

SPOOOOOKY!

IS ANYONE MORE QUALIFIED FOR THIS THAN MARTHA JONES?

AKA BIG TROUBLE.

NOT INCLUDING MADAME VASTRA. SHE INSISTED THAT I MENTION THAT.

I AM A SCHOOL TEACHER, YOU KNOW!

WHO IS THE DOCTOR?

Okay, this is where things get weird.

That man you're with, he's an alien and he's a Time Lord from the planet Gallifrey and he's over 2,000 years old!

TIME LORDS

He's from a proud race called the Time Lords. They're very clever and can travel through time and space. They're also a bit boring, so the Doctor ran off with a TARDIS!

HOME SWEET HOME

Gallifrey, the Doctor's home, was 250 million light-years away from Earth.

The Doctor believed it was destroyed in the Time War – a great big battle with the Daleks. But then the Doctor and a few other versions of himself stopped that from happening. So Gallifrey's out there. Somewhere.

HE CLAIMS THAT HE INVENTED THE YORKSHIRE PUDDING.

THE DOCTOR LIES! DON'T BELIEVE EVERYTHING HE SAYS.

HE HAD A CAR CALLED BESSIE.

BRILL BIOLOGY

Time Lords are very different from humans. For a start, they've got two hearts. And they can regenerate. That means that if they're seriously injured, they become a brand-new person. They'll look different and act different, but they're still the same. (I told you things were going to get weird!)

TOP TRAVEL

The Doctor travels in the TARDIS. That stands for TIME AND RELATIVE DIMENSION IN SPACE. You already know that it looks like an old 1960s police phone box and that it's bigger on the inside. Hopefully you've got over the shock of that by now.

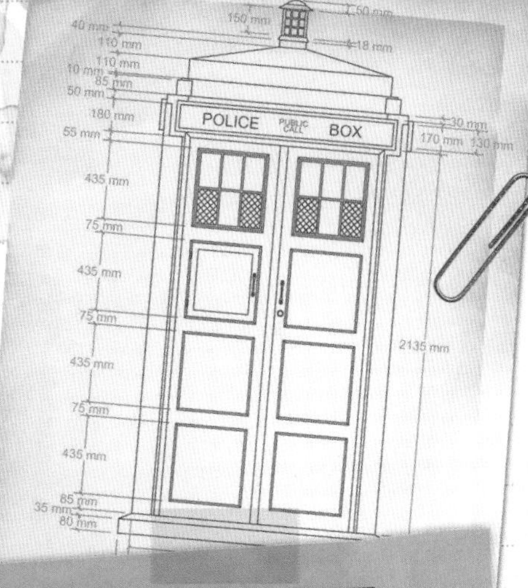

BIG BRAIN

The Doctor can speak over five billion languages, including horse, baby and dinosaur. He's not very good at talking to grown-up humans, though. He tells them they're boring and have wide faces.

TIME TRAINING

The Doctor went to the Time Lord Academy to learn all about the Laws of Time and lots of other important stuff he then decided to ignore. Newbies had to look into the Untempered Schism (at the very, very powerful Time Vortex). Some went mad. (Hello, Missy!) Some ran off. (Goodbye, Doctor!)

HE HAS A CLONE DAUGHTER CALLED JENNY.

DIFFERENT DOCTORS

Like I said: one man, many faces.
Here are all the versions of the Doctor – so far.

FIRST DOCTOR

1 Like a grumpy grandad!

SECOND DOCTOR

2 Could play the fool, but was still a hero.

THIRD DOCTOR

3 Liked gadgets, Venusian aikido and ruffles!

FOURTH DOCTOR

4 Big eyes. Big hair. Big scarf. Big brain.

FIFTH DOCTOR

5 The politest Doctor in all of time and space!

SIXTH DOCTOR

6 Thought he was a big deal. Loved garish clothes!

SEVENTH DOCTOR

7 Sometimes silly, sometimes a total control freak!

EIGHTH DOCTOR

8 This one was a bit of a romantic!

THE WAR DOCTOR

!

Had to be a warrior to end the Time War.

TENTH DOCTOR

10

Very funny, but could get very cross!

Allons-y!

NINTH DOCTOR

9

Rose Tyler taught him to laugh. He taught her to run.

Fantastic!

ELEVENTH DOCTOR

11

He really was a mad man with a box.

Geronimo!

TWELFTH DOCTOR

12

This grey-haired stick insect is ~~MY~~ YOUR Doctor!

THE TWELFTH DOCTOR

So here he is – your Doctor. The latest in a long line of the same amazing person. Here's what you need to know . . .

A BIT MORE ON THE ELEVENTH DOCTOR

Let's get this straight. I started travelling with this guy. He searched me out after meeting me a few times – we had a blast, and he wanted to find out more about me, his Impossible Girl.

This Doctor ended up on a planet called Trenzalore for about 900 years, defending the place from Daleks, Cybermen and all sorts of bad guys. He was trying to stop another Time War from happening (which is absolutely something everyone should do). He got old and was close to the end of his run, but I had a word with the Time Lords and they granted him more regenerations!

HE REGENERATED WITH A BOOM. WIPING OUT THE DALEKS AND BECOMING THIS GUY . . .

THE NEW DOCTOR

This wasn't the face I was expecting. To be honest, I don't think it's the kind of face anyone expects. It's the kind of face that just happens.

A DIFFICULT START

Right after he regenerated we lost control of the TARDIS, got swallowed by a dinosaur and then ended up in Victorian London. Not great, but at least the Paternoster Gang was there to help. The Doctor was super confused, but fighting some Clockwork Droids definitely helped sort him out.

At first I wasn't sure. Meeting a new version of the same person is tough, I won't deny it. But a call from an old friend was the reminder I needed that my job is to look after him.

TURN OVER! THERE'S MORE. THERE'S ALWAYS MORE!

Everything you need to know about the Twelfth Doctor:

He can look angry, but that doesn't mean he's angry.

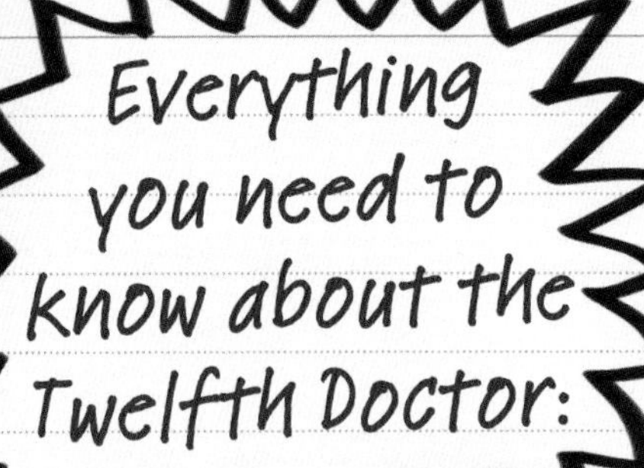

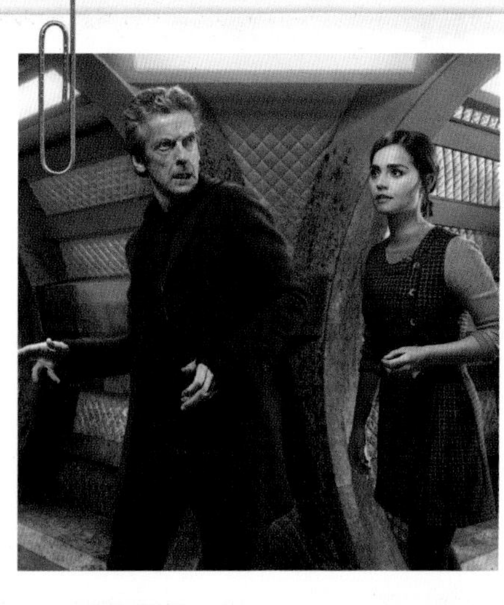

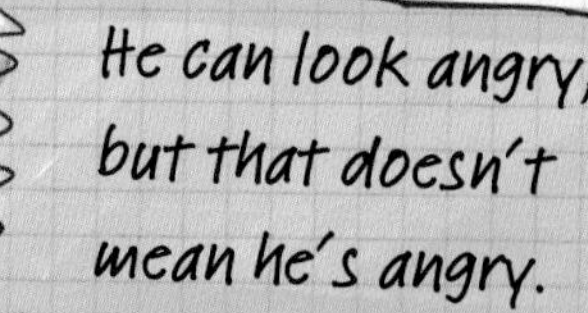

He can look angry, and sometimes it means he's really

ANGRY.

He doesn't like karaoke, mime or babysitters.

He likes books, blackboards and problems he can solve.

He's not the hugging type.

He says that his special power is 'taking charge'.

He likes lots of sugar in his tea.

He'll put himself in danger to protect those he cares about.

He'll put himself in danger to protect those he doesn't care about.

He tells a lot of people to

SHUT UP!

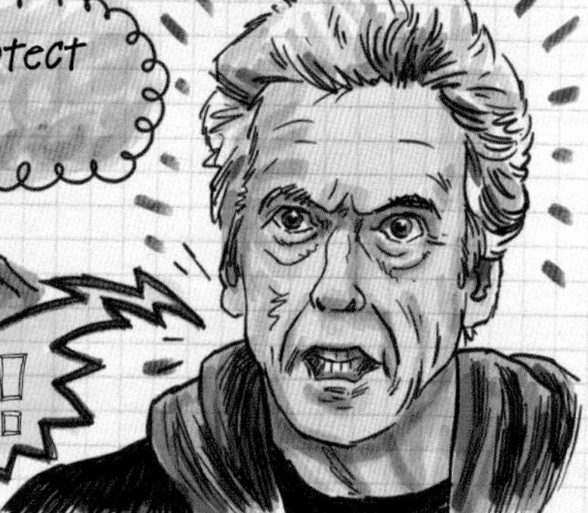

A FEW THINGS YOU DON'T NEED TO KNOW. BUT I THOUGHT I'D SHARE ANYWAY AS THEY'RE PRETTY IMPRESSIVE:

HE'S BEEN INSIDE A DALEK (although, so have I – more than once).

Once, the TARDIS started shrinking and he got stuck inside it!

He went undercover as a caretaker at Coal Hill School.

FACE FACTS

Just occasionally, the Doctor doesn't say what he's thinking. So here's a guide to what his different faces really mean. While he still has this face, that is. When it changes, you're on your own . . .

Listen Up!

Mr Time Lord has something very important to say, so pay attention! (You really should, because he'll say the most important things you've ever heard and they'll save your life.)

THE THINKER!

Is he pondering the great mysteries of the unknown universe? Is he planning on thwarting an evil Dalek invasion? Don't be fooled. He's trying to remember where he left the TARDIS.

HERE'S A CLUE: IT COULD BE ANYWHERE EVER!

THE COOL DUDE!

Sometimes you'll see the Doctor in his sonic shades. But other times he'll just be in a pair of normal ones. If he's looking cool, he's making an entrance. And if he's making an entrance, then whomever or whatever he's storming in on is in pretty big trouble!

CREEPED OUT!

This face means that something spooky is happening. It's a good time to check behind you. Or above you. Or below you. Be slow. Be careful. Be brave. If the Doctor's creeped out, then you know it's gonna get WEIRD fast!

As a rule, if the Doctor is running, then you should definitely be running. He might grab your hand – or you might grab his. That look on his face is all about getting you to safety, and it means business. You'll see it a lot, because you'll be running a lot!

Living proof that you can know everything and still get thrown by the smallest things. Sleet. Muffins. Unicorns. Even the Doctor gets confused, but he learns fast. And then teaches everyone else.

The Cool Dude 2!

Okay, this time he IS using the sonic sunglasses. He's tight-lipped and thinking as he scans away back there.

TOP TIP: KEEP AN EYE ON THOSE EYEBROWS. THE MORE THEY WIGGLE, THE MORE INFORMATION HE'S TRYING TO TAKE IN.

THE DOCTOR being . . . THE DOCTOR

Look at this. He looks terrifying. He's a healer and a warrior. A hero and a legend. He's ancient and brand new. This face means he's the Doctor.

I love this face.

SNIFFING

HE'S FIGURING STUFF OUT. OR HE CAN SMELL A PONGY SLITHEEN. IT MIGHT BE ON ANOTHER STREET OR ANOTHER PLANET, MIND!

TASTING

HE CAN TASTE WHERE AND WHEN HE IS. HANDY WHEN YOU REGULARLY LAND IN UNFAMILIAR PLACES.

LAUGHING

IT'S NOT A REGULAR OCCURRENCE, AND IT USUALLY HAPPENS OVER SOMETHING THAT YOU WON'T FIND FUNNY AT ALL . . .

FIRST THINGS FIRST!

Travelling with the Doctor? Then you need to do these

three things ASAP!

The TARDIS is a time-travelling vehicle that goes anywhere, anywhen, anyhow. It's bigger on the inside, but to get past the smaller bit you're going to need a key. And you're going to have to earn the Doctor's trust before you get it. Show him you're real. Show him you're brave. Show him you care.

The TARDIS is the safest place to be in the universe. Not because aliens can't get inside it, but because where you find the TARDIS is where you'll find the Doctor.

TOP TIP: Keep your phone away from Cybermen – they can use any tech to update themselves.

Number 2: GET BOOSTED!

Get the Doctor to use his sonic screwdriver on your phone, and you'll get a superphone . . . and Universal Roaming!

This means you can contact anyone you need to get hold of, even if they're on a normal, boring old phone on Earth.

Number 3: GET MOVING!

When you're with the Doctor, there's a lot of running. You'll be running from aliens, monsters and explosions. Oh, and did I mention robots? Yeah, you'll see plenty of them too.

If the Doctor stops running then that means there's going to be even more trouble.

YOU'LL BE ON THE MOVE A LOT, SO FOLLOW THESE TIPS:

- GET STRETCHING. YOU'LL NEED TO BE AS BENDY AS A BLATHEREEN.
- STAY HYDRATED. YOU BET YOU'LL SWEAT!
- GET SOME COMFY TRAINERS. YOU WON'T CARE ABOUT YOUR SHOES LOOKING GOOD WHEN YOU'RE ON THE RUN FROM AN ARMY OF ANGRY SONTARANS. (THIS WILL HAPPEN. PROBABLY ABOUT ONCE A WEEK.)

A HISTORY OF COMPANIONS

Getting info on all of the people who've travelled with the Doctor is pretty tough. Some only travelled with him for a day. Some travelled with him for a lifetime. And others did both simultaneously . . .

BIG THANKS TO THE OSGOODS AT UNIT FOR ACCESS TO THE BLACK ARCHIVE COMPANION FILES!

SUSAN FOREMAN

The Doctor's granddaughter. Yes! Granddaughter! She stopped travelling with him when she settled down with a guy on Earth. Where is she now, huh?

Love her styl

IAN CHESTERTON

Was Susan's teacher, and is now Chairman of Governors at Coal Hill School. So sort of my boss's boss's boss. Awkward!

Another Coal Hill teacher. Barbara was a history buff. Good job too – she went back in time a LOT.

What is it with the Doctor and teachers?

From the future, but ended up marrying a king's son and living in the past. Fancy!

STEVEN TAYLOR

Went from space-pilot prisoner to helper of humanity. Had a few clashes with the Doctor along the way.

Once a servant in Troy, she sacrificed herself during a Dalek ambush.

Daleks are DEADLY.

SARA KINGDOM

This brave Space Security Service agent was aged to death by a Dalek Time Destructor.

DODO

Dorothea Chaplet was sent off to rest after being brainwashed by a super-computer.

POLLY

She saw the Doctor regenerate, and did battle with War Machines and Cybermen!

BEN JACKSON

This sailor's shore leave got a lot more interesting when he fought aliens with the Doctor.

JAMIE MCCRIMMON

Jamie was a soldier and piper from the 1700s. The Time Lords returned him to the day he left, with his memory wiped.

VICTORIA WATERFIELD

She was orphaned when her dad was exterminated by the Daleks, so the Doctor looked after her. She ended up living with a new family on Earth.

ZOE HERIOT

This brainy astrophysicist met the Doctor in 2079. She was returned to her home by the Time Lords, also with her memory erased.

THE BRIGADIER

UNIT bigwig Alistair Gordon Lethbridge-Stewart helped the Doctor plenty of times – especially the Third Doctor, when he was exiled to Earth.

I met him. He was dead and he was a Cyberman, but he was still a hero.

LIZ SHAW

She assisted the Doctor with UNIT, but he was a bit bossy for her liking . . .

JO GRANT

Jo assisted the Third Doctor with UNIT. She ended up having an adventure with the Eleventh Doctor too!

SERGEANT BENTON

A UNIT Sergeant who got turned into a baby and back again! Oops!

CAPTAIN YATES

Mike Yates worked closely with the Brig, but left UNIT after being brainwashed and turning on his friends.

SARAH JANE SMITH

This brave journalist became one of the Doctor's best friends, and saw the creation of the Daleks.

THERE'S A LOT TO LEARN FROM THIS LADY!

HARRY SULLIVAN

A Lieutenant at UNIT, Harry travelled with the Fourth Doctor and Sarah. He left after becoming a Zygon prisoner.

LEELA

This warrior was determined that the Doctor should take her with him on his adventures! She eventually settled down on Gallifrey.

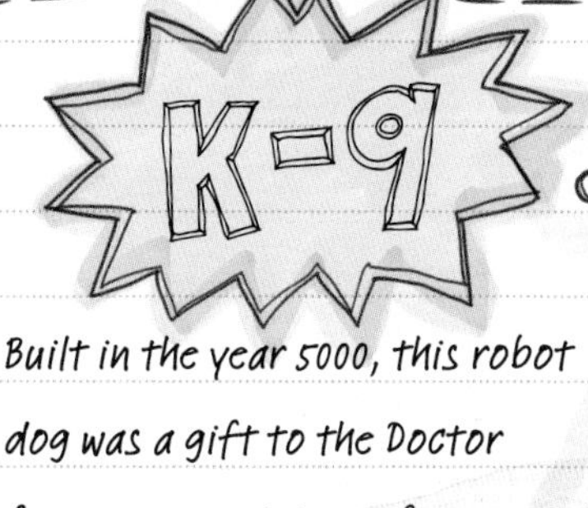

Built in the year 5000, this robot dog was a gift to the Doctor from an eccentric professor. There were four versions and they were all awesome!

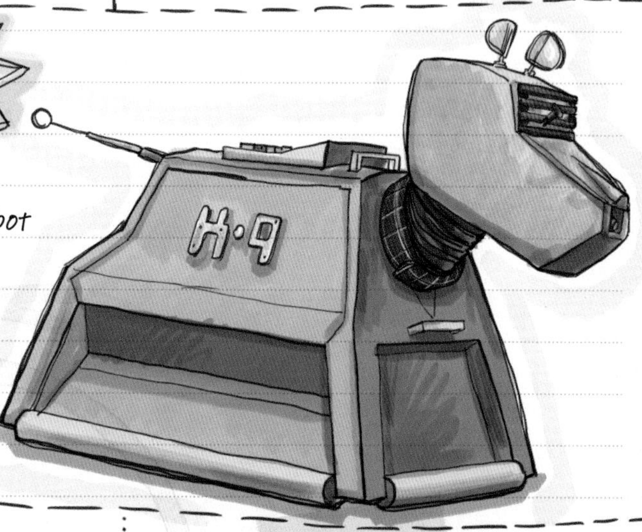

ROMANA I

Romanadvoratrelundar was a Time Lady who helped the Doctor find the scattered parts of the Key to Time. Then she regenerated!

ROMANA II

This incarnation of Romana was still super smart. She was called back home by the Time Lords, but ended up staying in a pocket universe.

THE DOCTOR SAID THIS ONE WA

ADRIC

Born on the planet Alzarius, this teen was a mathematician who fought the Master, Terileptils and Cybermen!

NYSSA

Nyssa was Traken nobility. She left the TARDIS to try and help find a cure for Lazar's Disease on Terminus.

TEGAN JOVANKA

On the way to her first day as an air stewardess, Tegan ended up in the TARDIS . . . and then on an alien planet!

VISLOR TURLOUGH

Turlough was taken over by the Black Guardian and told to kill the Doctor, but he didn't – he travelled with him instead.

KAMELION

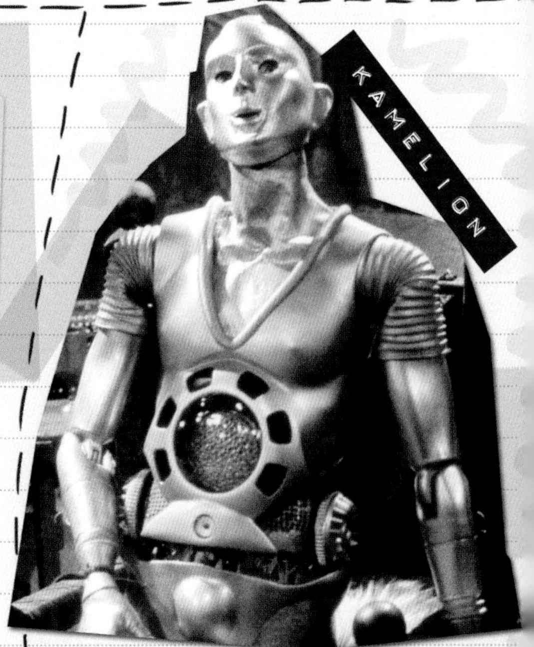

Amazing shape-shifting robot who kept getting controlled by the Master. Had to be destroyed. Very sad.

PERPUGILLIAM 'PERI' BROWN

Peri helped the Fifth Doctor battle the Master. Later they both got a weird disease on Androzani Minor; the Doctor managed to save her but then he had to regenerate.

MELANIE BUSH

She had a timey-wimey out-of-order adventure with the Doctor. She battled the Rani and old ladies that tried to eat her!

ACE

The Doctor rescued Dorothy (don't call her that, though!) from Iceworld. Then he made her face her greatest fears.

GOOD JOB SHE WAS SO BRAVE!

GRACE HOLLOWAY

This American doctor tried to save the Seventh Doctor, but that didn't go to plan. Then she helped the Eighth Doctor stop the Master!

ROSE TYLER

An Auton attack in her shop led Rose to a troubled Ninth Doctor – and a life of adventure. She nearly wiped out all the Daleks!

BASICALLY, SHE'S A LEGEND!

MICKEY SMITH

Rose's boyfriend went from 'Mickey the Idiot' to Cyberman-battling hero on a parallel Earth.

CAPTAIN JACK

I'VE HEARD HE LIVES ON

Rose Tyler used the power of the Time Vortex to bring this Time Agent back to life – and now he can't die. He joined Torchwood and has been getting into all sorts of trouble ever since.

MARTHA JONES

When her hospital was taken to the moon by Judoon, this medical student met the Tenth Doctor. She's now a doctor and has worked for UNIT and Torchwood.

DONNA NOBLE

After an adventure with the Doctor on her wedding day, Donna sought him out so she could travel with him. She became part Time Lord after a battle with Davros, but she had to have her mind wiped to save her life.

ASTRID PETH

Astrid was a waitress on the doomed Titanic starliner. She helped the Doctor defeat Max Capricorn and save Earth. She's stardust now, travelling the galaxy as she'd always dreamed of doing.

WILFRED MOTT

Donna's grandad helped the Doctor battle the Master and the Time Lords. While saving Wilfred, the Tenth Doctor was exposed to radiation and had to regenerate.

AMY POND

After his regeneration, the Eleventh Doctor's TARDIS crashed in Amelia Pond's garden. She waited twelve years for him to return, and then travelled with him and her boyfriend, Rory.

RORY WILLIAMS

Amy's boyfriend joined the TARDIS team and died a lot, but he came back a lot too. As an Auton Roman Centurion, he guarded Amy in the Pandorica for 2,000 years.

THIS GUY WAS A KEEPER, AND AMY KNEW IT TOO!

RIVER SONG

Amy and Rory's daughter was taken by the Silence and raised to kill the Doctor. They both ended up sort of dying and sort of getting married. She joined him for various adventures in between.

THE ONLY THING BIGGER THAN RIVER'S PERSONALITY WAS HER HAIR!

THE PATERNOSTER GANG

A trio of Victorian crime-fighting heroes – Madame Vastra the Silurian, Jenny Flint (her wife) and Commander Strax the Sontaran. They teamed up to help the Doctor.

SLIGHTLY WEIRD, FULLY WONDERFUL.

CRAIG OWENS

The Eleventh Doctor moved into Craig's flat and they discovered an alien spaceship upstairs! Then Craig and the Doctor stopped a Cyberman invasion. Craig blew them up with love. Awww.

OSWIN

According to the Doctor, this version of me was a Junior Entertainment Officer on the crashed starship *Alaska*. She guided him, Amy and Rory through the Dalek Asylum. But they were too late to help her – she'd been turned into a Dalek.

VICTORIAN CLARA

A posh governess by day and a barmaid by night, this Clara tried to keep the kids she looked after away from the Ice Governess and the Great Intelligence's Snowmen. Sounds fun!

Ta-da! This is me. After meeting Oswin and Victorian Clara, the Doctor came looking for me. Just in time, because I was getting uploaded into the Cloud, thanks to the Great Intelligence. I was there when the Doctor regenerated into the man he is today!

ALL ABOUT ALIENS : DALEKS

I'm getting straight to the point here. The Daleks are the worst. They corrupt. They destroy. They know only hate. Meet your deadliest enemies . . .

WHAT ARE THEY?

They're squashy mutants inside deadly tanks, and they want to EXTERMINATE everything. They have deadly blasters and deadly plungers. I know I'm using the word deadly a lot, but I'm trying to make a point here.

The Daleks were created by a Kaled scientist called Davros. When the Thals were at war with the Kaleds, and radiation from the war was turning the Kaleds into mutants, Davros created mega-tanks to keep the mutated Kaleds safe. He's very cruel and very clever.

The Doctor and I ended up inside a Dalek once. Seeing a Dalek from the inside is just as scary as seeing one from the outside, in case you were wondering. They're full of goo, laser-shooting antibodies and very bad feelings.

Rose Tyler absorbed the power of the Time Vortex and used it to wipe out most of the Daleks. No pressure – not all companions are expected to save the universe. (We do seem to do it a lot, though.)

HOW TO HELP THE DOCTOR DEFEAT THEM:

THIS ONE'S EASY. YOU DO WHATEVER THE DOCTOR SAYS. YOU NEVER REALLY DEFEAT THE DALEKS, YOU JUST ESCAPE THEM. AND THEN YOU LIVE ON AND MAKE EVERY SINGLE DAY COUNT.

The Doctor is going to be scared, and that will make you feel even more scared. So you're going to have to be twice as brave and run twice as fast.

DONNA'S DIARY

She's a wonderful girl, my Donna. A real character. Travelling with the Doctor definitely brought out the best in her.

But then she had to forget it all.

She kept a diary of her amazing adventures, but I had to take it from her. It's so worth sharing, though – it's <u>so</u> Donna.

Wilf Mott

Saturday 12th Spent most of the day on the run from some VERY angry weasel creatures. APPARENTLY they were angry because I called them weasel creatures, when they are, in fact, THE YUVERIAN ROYAL FAMILY! Whoops! That's so me, right? The Doctor pretended that I'd nearly caused a galactic civil war, but I did catch him smiling a few times. I put everything right by treating everyone to coffee. Totally wizard!

Sunday 13th

WHAT A DAY! Well, two days. From three days ago. It's hard to keep a diary when you're travelling through time and space. And I know a thing or two about administration, what with me being the best temp in Chiswick! I reminded Alien Boy that we'd still not been to the PLANET OF THE HATS, and we ended up visiting the PLANET OF THE BATS. Not as much fun as it sounds. Hair in v. v. v. bad condition.

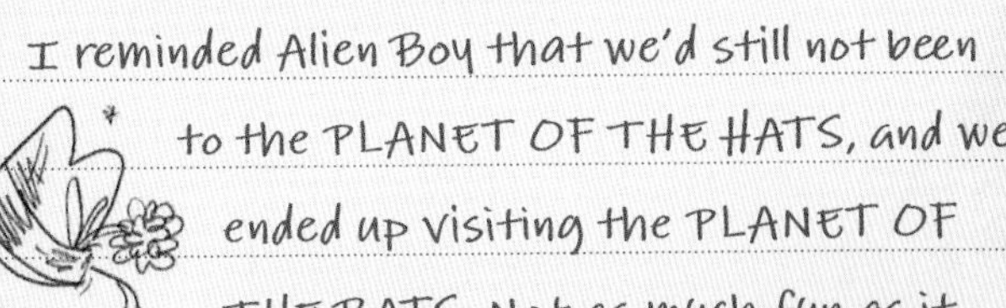

Monday 14th

Took charge of the TARDIS today. That SKINNY BOY told me to give it a go, and you'll never guess what happened! I only went and landed her right on the BIGGEST SHOPPING CENTRE IN THE UNIVERSE. Nerys would be sooo jealous. When I was looking for bargain accessories, the Doctor managed to thwart a full-scale invasion from an army of possessed shoes. He's brilliant, isn't he?

Nerys

~~Tuesday 15th~~ Monday 14th

I've had a lot of Mondays lately. But that's okay because Mondays aren't about going back to school or work. It's not the start of the week – it's the start of a new adventure. With my old bestie, the Doctor. The TARDIS received a distress signal and we set off to help. 'HELP' and 'ME' are the two words he can't turn his back on. He saved a family of Wapplebung travellers from a meat tornado. When he can help, he does. When he can't, then he's got me to remind him that he can.

Wednesday 25th

Left him off on his own today, so MOI got some time to be totally pampered. The Doctor likes to look at rocks and I'm more about lying by a pool being served drinks by alien waiters. My waiter said he had 250 brothers. I asked if they were all as handsome as him and he said yes – they're from a clone batch. Turns out that his clone batch was captured by some sort of space war lord, so as soon as the Doctor was back we went and rescued 250 handsome alien waiters. They were very grateful.

Thursday 26th

Great! Only went and got kidnapped again, didn't I? That is so TYPICAL.

Mr Stripy Suit was distracted with some gadget or other and then I end up in the back of a disgusting old spaceship. It was filthy and I told them so. I told them they could do with getting a rag round their windows and some nice flooring down and sorting out the creaks. They said I wouldn't stop talking and dropped me back. RUDE! The Doctor didn't even notice I'd gone. RUDER!

Friday 27th

Found amazing planet with a sea made out of gold. Not kidding. Actual gold! It was beautiful. Just when I thought it couldn't get any better, it turns out they had a FREE MARKET. You could take whatever you wanted. FOR FREE! I picked up an amazing telescope for Gramps. He will love it. Later on, I learned that FREEMARKET translates as very expensive, rare vintage goods that are definitely not free for the taking.

OOPS!

Saturday 28th

Sort of got lost in the TARDIS for most of the day. Might have been longer than a day, actually. I found the library (someone needs to put those books in order), a kitchen, a swimming pool, a swimming pool on the ceiling, a room dedicated to oil paintings of cats, and a garage. I was pretty angry for the first few hours, but by the end of it I was running around laughing, like some kind of MANIAC. I love this.

I love <u>all</u> of it.

MEOW-NA LISA!

Monday 1st

Back to Earth to catch up with Mum and Wilf. Mum really is not a big fan of the Doctor. She made him a cup of tea, but no biscuits. Luckily, Gramps sneaked him some biscuits when she wasn't looking.

She's never liked my best friends. She thought Julie was common and Tanya had small eyes. She didn't like Nerys either, but then again no one does. But the Doctor is more than that. He's not just the most amazing person I've ever met – he makes me feel like I'm amazing too.

Tuesday 2nd

Running ALL day. Honestly, there's no need to pay for a gym membership when you're with Old Long Legs. We got chased by robots, which isn't fair, because they don't get tired. The Doctor had this amazing idea, so we ran outside in the wind and the rain. The robots got rusty pretty quick and stopped chasing us. However, what SPACE GENIUS didn't count on was me getting a STINKING COLD. He did make me some hot chocolate, though, so he's forgiven!

Wednesday 3rd

You ever get that feeling that big things are coming? Dangerous and amazing things? You feel scared about them, but then excited, because you wouldn't have it any other way. That's what travelling with the Doctor's like. Everything that should be impossible is possible. Not because of the TARDIS. Not because of the aliens. None of that. Just because you have your best mate by your side.

FRIDAY 12TH

Boring day as usual. Nothing to report – nothing exciting ever happens here, does it?

TARDIS TRAVEL ESSENTIALS!

PART ONE

PYJAMAS

Not every trip in the TARDIS is a short one. There will be times when you'll be going from adventure to adventure without stopping, or you'll get stranded somewhere for ages. You'll be glad of some comfy pyjamas if you're trapped in Earth's Stone Age or have to sleep in a bed made out of pineapples (it happens).

SPOTS OR STRIPES ARE FINE!

NO EXCUSE FOR SLIPPERS, THOUGH. CAN'T RUN FAST IN THOSE!

JELLY BABIES

These were a favourite of the Fourth Doctor. He carried them with him at all times and used them to trick, tease and tempt all sorts of aliens. I keep them with me because they're a good source of energy – perfect for keeping me running.

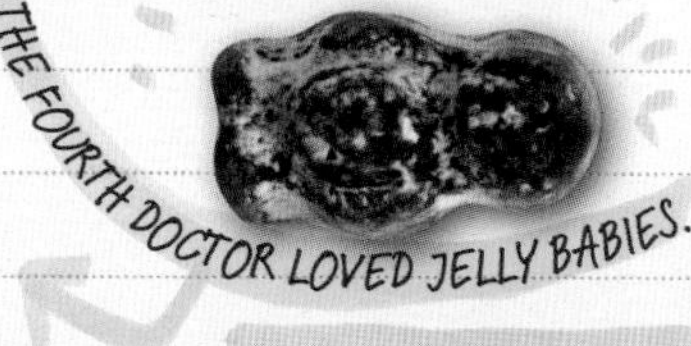

THE FOURTH DOCTOR LOVED JELLY BABIES.

MOBILE PHONE

I've already told you that you need to get your phone boosted by the Doctor so you can make calls across time and space. If things start to seem really alien, then you might need to catch up with your family and friends. Stay as human as possible. Stay as YOU as possible. Also DO NOT miss the chance to get a selfie on the Lost Moon of Poosh!

SLIME REMOVER

FACT 1
YOU WILL RUN A LOT.

FACT 2
YOU WILL BE IN DANGER A LOT.

FACT 3
YOU WILL LAUGH A LOT.

FACT 4
YOU WILL GET COVERED IN SLIME A LOT.

VERY VERY IMPORTANT!

SLIME-O-WAY

SORRY, GOT SLIME EVERYWHERE . . .

It might be from the frothy fronds of an Ood with red-eye or some good old Ganger goo, but you will definitely get splattered with slime. You can wash it off your hands easily enough, but you might need some help getting it off your clothes!

HOW TO SOLVE A MYSTERY IN FIVE STEPS!

You'll need to know how to find clues, follow leads and solve mysteries when you travel with the Doctor.

1. TALK TO EVERYONE!

First things first, you need to talk to as many people as possible.

The Doctor can be a bit . . . moody, so often it's your job to be the kind one. Remember aliens and monsters have feelings too. So be nice to everyone. Even if they have three heads. ESPECIALLY if they have three heads.

2. USE YOUR EYES!

We're not all as clever as the Doctor, so work hard to spot everything. What's the weather like? Is it raining? Is the rain going up or down? Is the floor wet? Does anyone have an umbrella? Is that umbrella an alien weapon? Keep asking yourself questions like these.

Just because the Doctor is super clever doesn't mean he sees everything. There are simple patterns and behaviours he might miss – he tends to think of the most complicated option!

3. RESEARCH!

Okay, people don't like homework. Nobody knows that better than me. However, doing your research and finding the right information is key to solving a mystery.

The Doctor likes to set up a few hundred blackboards and do sums and write down hypothetical equations . . . yawn. I tend to go online and see what I can find there.

4. THINK LOGICALLY!

Then think weirdly!

'If it walks like a duck and quacks like a duck, then it's probably a duck!' says my nan. Look for the most obvious answer first, as it's often the right one.

However, it could be a Zygon disguised as a duck. Or it could be an uprising of ducks – they're evolving and becoming telepathic, they're bored of bread and want revenge – THEY COULD BE COMING FOR ALL OF US . . . Wow. I got a bit carried away there. Maybe I'm going quackers.

5. LET THE DOCTOR DO HIS THING!

Let him taste the air, talk to babies and absorb every bit of the situation. Watch his eyebrows dance as he unravels the mysteries of time, questions the building blocks of humanity, remembers ancient bus timetables for parts of North Birmingham and scans everything with his sonic screwdriver.

He needs you while he's doing all that stuff. You'll need to be there to bounce ideas off, to share intriguing thoughts with and to get a talking-to.

ALL ABOUT ALIENS: SILENTS

How can you fight something you can't remember? These telepathic terrors were part of a massive plan to stop the Doctor and his companions Amy and Rory.

WHAT ARE THEY?

The Silence are a religious movement – and these creepy bulb-heads are a part of it. They're genetically engineered priests with the power to make people confess their sins and then forget all about it. These guys have telepathic powers, can use electricity to make people pop, AND you completely forget when you've seen them.

Amy, Rory and River had a tough time in the 1960s – they had to go on the run from the FBI and loads of Silents. They marked their skin every time they saw a sneaky Silent (a lot).

River Song was taken from Amy and Rory by the Silence and raised to kill the Doctor. But River, being River, didn't do what she was told. Which made time and space go all weird, but as always the Doctor had a sort-of plan to put things right.

I can just about remember meeting Silents. During the Siege of Trenzalore, some Silents became Dalek puppets – complete with eyestalks sticking out of their egg-heads.

HOW TO HELP THE DOCTOR DEFEAT THEM:

Some Silents are very tricky and love manipulating people and time and, well . . . everything. Follow your instincts and be wary. Amy and Rory's idea of drawing tallies on themselves is a good one – that way you'll have proof that you've seen a Silent even once you've forgotten.

HOW TO PRETEND YOU DON'T TRAVEL IN TIME AND SPACE

Sometimes it's safer for everyone if they don't know about your journeys with the Doctor. Here are some tips on how to answer those tricky questions.

'WHY ARE YOU DRESSED LIKE THAT?'

This look is totally coming back. You could say I'm a trendsetter. In fact, I DID set this trend, in the 1920s. Ha, ha. Just kidding. I am absolutely NOT a time-traveller.

I'm going to a fancy-dress party! They're a right laugh, aren't they? What? No, you haven't been invited. Shame. See ya.

I'm doing a project for school. Or: All my other clothes were in the wash. Or: I think it's going to rain later and nothing keeps you dry like an astronaut suit.

QUICK-FIRE ANSWERS:

'YOU LOOK OLDER . . .'

- I AM older. We're all older. Even after a second we're all a second older.
- How dare you! I've never been so offended. (Walk off, frowning furiously.)
- Maybe you're just getting younger? (Walk off, laughing loudly.)

'WHY DO I KEEP FINDING PICTURES OF YOU IN HISTORY BOOKS?'

- I just have one of those faces.
- I come from a long line of kings / queens / warriors / inventors.
- Why do you keep reading history books? Live in the now!

HOW TO ADMIT YOU TRAVEL IN TIME AND SPACE!

Okay, it isn't easy telling your family and friends that you're a time-travelling space hero and that your best friend is well over 2,000 years old. Here's a handy letter.

Dear MUM / DAD / BROTHER / SISTER / NEIGHBOUR/ CLASSMATE / PARTNER / DENTIST*

As you know, my name is ______________________.

You have mentioned that lately I am ALWAYS LATE / ALWAYS EARLY / ALWAYS COVERED IN WEIRD GOO / ALWAYS LISTENING FOR A 'WHEEZING SOUND'*.

What I am about to tell you is very unusual, but please listen and trust me. I've met someone AMAZING / INTERESTING / TERRIFYING / BIG-HEADED*. He is called the Doctor. He is an alien with a spaceship that travels through time.

I met the Doctor a few HOURS / DAYS / WEEKS / YEARS / LIFETIMES* ago and have decided that I want to travel with him. You know how much I like ADVENTURES / FUN / EXPLORING / MEETING NEW PEOPLE / DANGER* so I hope you agree that this is the right choice for me.

I want you to know that I will do everything I can to be safe and sensible, probably, most of the time. Just don't act surprised if:

- You see me go into a blue box that disappears.
- I pop up in ancient epic poems, old films or on alien currency.
- I forget birthdays or celebrate them forty-five times.

Just remember I LOVE YOU / LIKE YOU / CARE FOR YOU / RESPECT YOU / THINK YOU'RE SORT OF ALL RIGHT*.

Yours sincerely,

*delete as appropriate

POND MAIL

Here's an extract from one of Amy Pond's letters, talking about the Doctor.

New York,
New York, USA
23 November 1963

When a weird crack appeared in my bedroom wall, I did the only sensible thing and prayed to Santa to send help. And there he was – the Doctor.

He taught me all about life and fish fingers and custard. Then he was off again. He kept me waiting. A LOT. I mean, seriously. I was waiting for my Raggedy Man to show up for over twelve years. Okay, so it made me very angry . . . and a little bitey . . . but I got over it. He returned.

I saved a whale in outer space, went to sea and fought pirates, and fell in love with a man who waited 2,000 years to keep me safe. I've lived in dream worlds and alternative universes. I've had my socks washed by an Ood. I've been chased by dinosaurs.

I waited another thirty-six years.

I didn't just find adventure – I found a family. I married Rory and we had a daughter, Melody Pond, who became River Song, who became a legend.

My Doctor was so young and so old. He walked like a goat on stilts and danced like a drunk giraffe. He found delight in the simplest of things and simplicity in the most complex of things.

When I was taken from him, he went to war.

And now? Well, Rory and I are here. And the Doctor's there. So in many ways I'll always be waiting. But waiting doesn't mean standing still – oh, no. Once you've spent all that time running, you can't go back to standing still. We live and love and find our adventures in everything here. And we hope the Doctor's as happy as we are.

amy x

SONIC SHADES AND SCREWDRIVERS

The Doctor has a thing about sonic devices – you know, things that operate on soundwaves. Normally, he uses a sonic screwdriver, but then that got too normal for a while, so he started using some other variants!

SONIC SHADES

If you think sunglasses make you look cool, then you're right. Especially when it comes to this pair. Featuring all of the Doctor's fancy Time Lord tech and super-sonic stuff, these shades sit handily on your nose.

GREAT FOR:

- Calling the TARDIS.
- Connecting to Wi-Fi.
- Unlocking chains and vans.
- Examining holograms and aliens.

TERRIBLE FOR:

- Overcast British weather.
- Aliens without ears, noses or eyes.
- Storing browsing history.

SONIC SCREWDRIVER

This is the tool most often used by the Doctor. I love the fact that he has a screwdriver. What else would you expect from the man who tries to fix everything? This handy gadget has many functions, but you can't wear it in the sunshine. Sonic sunglasses win on that one.

GREAT FOR:

- Making star whales puke.
- Dissolving Gangers.
- Opening doors that should probably stay closed.
- Creating / blocking / boosting signals.
- Sending aliens back to their own universe.

TERRIBLE FOR:

- Anything wooden.
- Deadlocks.

OTHER SONICS:

The Eleventh Doctor got fancy and made a fancy sonic cane to match his fancy suit!

When Amy Pond was abandoned on Apalapucia, she built her own sonic probe!

The Tenth Doctor gave Sarah Jane Smith a sonic lipstick. I wouldn't mind one of these myself!

CARE CARDS

He's brilliant. He's a genius. He's a problem-solver. He's a hero. He's . . . terrible at talking to people.

The adventures you'll have with the Doctor will be very real. Real people. Real loss. Real life. You'll need to remind him to be kind. I produced these handy prompt cards to help him out.

I'M VERY SORRY FOR YOUR LOSS. I'LL DO ALL I CAN TO SOLVE THE DEATH OF YOUR FRIEND / FAMILY MEMBER / PET.

I COMPLETELY UNDERSTAND WHY IT WAS DIFFICULT NOT TO GET CAPTURED.

I DIDN'T
MEAN TO IMPLY
THAT I DON'T CARE.

IT WAS
MY FAULT, I SHOULD
HAVE KNOWN
YOU DIDN'T LIVE IN
ABERDEEN.

NO ONE IS GOING TO BE
EATEN / VAPOURISED /
EXTERMINATED / UPGRADED /
POSSESSED / MORTALLY
WOUNDED / TURNED TO JELLY.
WE'LL ALL GET OUT OF
THIS UNHARMED.

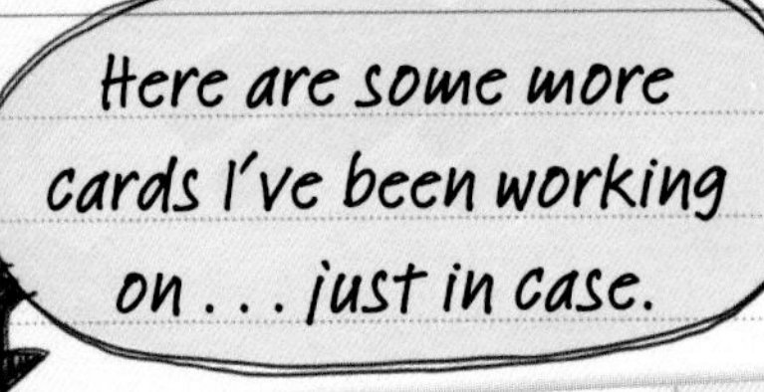

I'M VERY SORRY FOR SAYING THAT YOU HAVE A WIDE FACE. YOUR FACE AND YOUR HEAD ARE COMPLETELY IN PROPORTION WITH THE REST OF YOU.

I APOLOGISE FOR STEALING YOUR HORSE. IT WAS AN EMERGENCY. I WAS TRYING TO CHASE AFTER AN ALIEN / ESCAPE FROM AN ALIEN / SHOW AN ALIEN HOW TO RIDE A HORSE / SAVE YOU FROM YOUR HORSE BECAUSE YOUR HORSE IS AN ALIEN.

I WISH TO EXPRESS MY DEEP REGRET FOR LANDING MY TARDIS IN YOUR GARDEN. I NOW KNOW THAT IT WAS A MUCH-LOVED AND WELL-CULTIVATED OUTDOOR SPACE AND NOT 'A BIT OF SCRUFFY GRASS WITH SOME COLOURFUL BITS ON IT'.

IOU ONE GNOME.

I DIDN'T MEAN TO CALL YOU A WHIMPERING CRYBABY, WHEN YOU ARE IN FACT ONLY TWO YEARS OLD, AND ALLOWED TO CRY AS MUCH AS YOU LIKE.

I APOLOGISE IN ADVANCE FOR WHAT'S ABOUT TO HAPPEN. THAT MAY INCLUDE ONE OR ALL OF THE FOLLOWING:

- YOU BEING ATTACKED BY A MONSTER.
- YOU BEING KIDNAPPED BY A MONSTER.
- YOU BECOMING A MONSTER.
- YOU BEING TOLD OFF FOR MAKING A MONSTER SAD.
- A MONSTER EATING YOUR FRIEND ANDREW – THE ONE WITH THE SPIKY HAIR AND THE GLASSES. YOU KNOW THE ONE.

TRAVEL IN THE TARDIS

I'm not even going to try and tell you about controlling the TARDIS – that's for the Doctor to worry about. I'm going to give you my top tips on just being inside the TARDIS. It's not as easy as it sounds . . .

TARDIS FACTS

- It's got a Chameleon Circuit that can make the outside look like different things. The Doctor says it's broken, but personally I think he's just fond of the blue-box look.

- The inside of the TARDIS can change style or design at the Doctor's bidding. He keeps the old console rooms in an archive.

- This is a Type 40 TARDIS, which means it's an antique by Time Lord standards. Imagine what a new TARDIS is like!

The TARDIS did not like me to start off with. I was too much of a mystery – the Impossible Girl, and all that. But we soon got over that and we've been pals ever since. Here are a few things to be aware of:

Aliens called the Boneless once shrank the TARDIS with the Doctor inside. If things start to get shrinky, then you need to get out!

The TARDIS went bonkers when it had a run-in with a magno-grab. Lots of strange time stuff happened – including Time Zombies. They were fried versions of our future selves, and super creepy.

An evil force called House lured the TARDIS on to an asteroid using Time Lord distress signals, because he wanted to slurp the TARDIS's energy. He took over the TARDIS and trapped Amy and Rory inside with a possessed Ood called Nephew.

TURN OVER FOR A COMPLETELY USELESS MAP OF THE TARDIS.

Okay, I gave it my best shot. Here's a map of the inside of the TARDIS. But it does move around inside, and sometimes it changes its mind about where certain rooms should go. So it's probably only about two per cent accurate. Anyway, you're welcome.

Room with bunk beds
Romana's private study
The observatory
The Eye of Harmony
The TARDIS's power source!
Once found some bagpipes here
Garage
K-9's kennel
Hole in wall (created by Ace)
The Architectural Reconfiguration System
Secret power supply here!
Bathrooms 373-373
The swimming pool
ZOO
Sarah Jane Smith's writing room

UNIT
DR-19042
RL 10

UNIT REPORT 'THE DOCTOR'

Ref: 78/96206

A PERSONAL STATEMENT BY DR MARTHA JONES

Explain the Doctor? You ask me to explain the Doctor and you give me just two pieces of paper? I've had some challenges in my life, but this might be the biggest one yet.

Where shall I start? He's a Time Lord. He has a binary vascular system, lower body temperature and higher tolerance to radiation than a human male, and a respiratory bypass system. But I don't think you want a medical report, do you?

Okay, it all started when I was training to be a doctor. The hospital where I was studying was put on the moon by the Judoon. The Doctor was there and we worked together to sort it all out, then he promised me a single trip in the TARDIS. The rest is history, as they say . . .

I battled witches with Shakespeare, got cloned by Sontarans, visited New New York and old New York and was sent back in time by the touch of a Weeping Angel. Loved it. All of it.

When the Doctor hid from the Family of Blood by becoming human I stayed at his side, disguised as a servant. And when he was captured by the Master I travelled the Earth for a year to tell his story. Those were tough times - tough for a lot of people.

The Doctor I knew wore stripy suits and sand shoes. He felt the burden of being the last of the Time Lords and didn't want to be on his own.

When you're with the Doctor you try to be as good as him - you try to think as hard and run as fast. But you can't do that - nobody can. You just have to think about being the best you you can be. Because that's perfect. That's plenty.

Whoever is with him now should remember that.

Dr.M.Jones

THIS IS AN INTELL

CASE NUMBER 200.113

U.N.I.T.

U.N

SERIAL : 00653053 //8

LOTS OF DOCTORS!

You're going to be told all sorts of important stuff about not crossing time streams or altering the course of history. So you'll know that when Doctors clash, we're all in trouble!

OPERATION OMEGA

The First, Second and Third Doctors were all caught up in Time Lord Omega's evil plan. Omega had once worked to harness time-travelling power for the Time Lords, but got blasted to an antimatter universe and then fought hard to return again. These Doctors worked together and stopped him.

DEATH ZONE

The first five Doctors and loads of their companions were taken to Gallifrey and placed in the Death Zone. It was all part of a plan by a corrupt Time Lord president who wanted to become immortal. He didn't stand a chance against all five of these brilliant Doctors and their friends, though! (Also, who builds something called the Death Zone? You're asking for trouble.)

SONTARAN SCARES

The Second and Sixth Doctors joined forces to battle Sontarans and alien cannibals when the Time Lords sent them to investigate time-travel experiments. Can you imagine our Doctor doing anything he was ordered to do? No, nor can I!

TITANIC TIME CRASH

Just before the Tenth Doctor's TARDIS got bashed by the Titanic, he ran into the Fifth Doctor. Their time streams clashed and it threatened to rip a hole in time and space the size of Belgium. (I've been there for the weekend, and it's pretty big!) But they managed to sort the problem out and go on their sort-of-separate ways.

SAVING GALLIFREY

ALL of the Doctors turned up to help save Gallifrey from the Daleks and the Time War! Every existing version of the Doctor appeared in his TARDIS and used stasis-cube Time Lord technology to freeze Gallifrey in a pocket universe, rather than use the Moment to destroy it.

MOST WANTED (PART ONE)

You're going to meet a lot of aliens on your travels and the Doctor won't always be with you, so look at these faces (for the ones that have faces) and remember they're trouble!

Slitheen

The Slitheen are a big green criminal family from Raxacoricofallapatorius. They look out for big humans and turn them into skin suits – nasty! But the compression collars they use for this make them trump loads. You can smell these pongers from the other side of the galaxy.

Adipose

The Tenth Doctor and Donna had to deal with these little guys. They look fairly harmless, but they're made from fat – and that can be human fat. If a whole group of these turn up and lots of humans disappear, then there's slim chance they're innocent.

Sandmen

You know that crusty stuff you get in the corners of your eyes – well these guys are made out of that! Gross, right? The Doctor and I stopped these creatures reaching Earth, so no need to lose any sleep over them. At least, I think we stopped them . . .

The Foretold

The Foretold was an old soldier who looked like a mummy. If one of these ever turns up again, just hope that you have more than sixty-six seconds to do something about it – because that's how long you get between seeing it and dying.

Sycorax

An ugly bunch! These warriors use blood magic to control enemies. They're pretty handy with a sword – one of them cut off the Tenth Doctor's hand on Christmas Day. I've had some weird Christmases, but that sounds pretty bad!

WHO CAN HELP? PART 1: UNIT

Sometimes you're going to need help, and these are the people to turn to. It's not often the Doctor goes to UNIT – it's usually the other way round. But then he does work for them (long story).

WHO ARE UNIT?

UNIT stands for Unified Intelligence Taskforce. They're like a secret army that deals with weird stuff and aliens.

HOW CAN THEY HELP?

Well, they're an army – so they're pretty useful when you need manpower. They're there for the large-scale problems – invasions, worldwide phenomena, mysterious portals.

LET THEM:

- Track down the Doctor if he goes missing (unless he wants to be missing, then make up an excuse for him).
- Share their scientific resources – they've got some powerful minds on their team.

DON'T LET THEM:

- Shoot first and ask questions afterwards. The Doctor doesn't tend to like soldiers and weapons.
- Take control. The Doctor is always in charge. Though he doesn't like it when they make him President of Earth.

WHO'S WHO AT UNIT?

BRIGADIER LETHBRIDGE-STEWART

The Doctor talks very fondly about this soldier. When Missy turned the Earth's dead into Cybermen, the Cyber-converted Brigadier saved his daughter and stopped the crazy Time Lady.

OSGOODS

Petronella Osgood is a UNIT scientist and a big fan of the Doctor! Basically there are two of her. One or more of the Osgoods might be Zygon. This is a good thing because it helps keep the peace between Zygons and humans. Plus, they're brilliant, so two of them means twice as much brain power.

KATE STEWART

The Brigadier's daughter Kate is Head of Scientific Research at UNIT. She's dealt with the Shakri, Zygons, Cybermen, and much more. She's level-headed and smart, which are both pretty important characteristics for someone who controls an army.

MARTHA JONES

After travelling with the Doctor, Martha Jones became a doctor and joined UNIT! You go, Doctor Jones!

ALL ABOUT ALIENS: DREAM CRABS

Ever had a dream about a dream that you've been dreaming about? Confused? You will be. These creatures put you into a dream state while they turn your brain into a tasty drink.

WHAT ARE THEY?

They're actually called the Kantrofarri. Not that knowing that helped me when I came across them. They jump on you and grab on to your head; you then start dreaming as these guys basically eat your brains.

The Doctor and I ended up at the North Pole when a bunch of these creepy creatures latched on to a group of scientists. Turns out they weren't scientists. Nor were we at the North Pole. It was just a big shared dream.

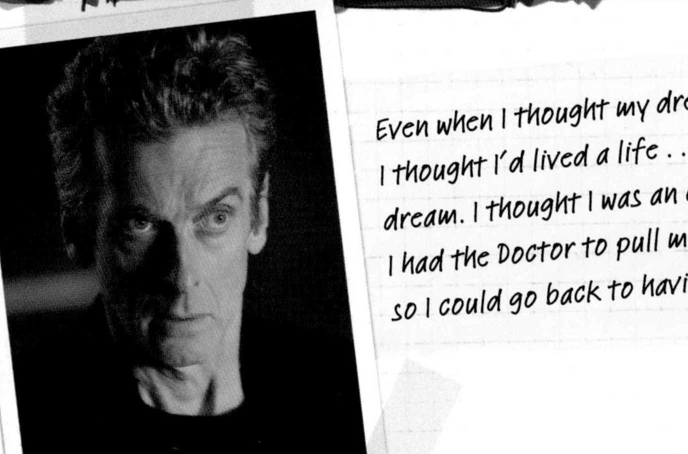

Even when I thought my dream was over, when I thought I'd lived a life . . . I was still in a dream. I thought I was an old woman. Luckily, I had the Doctor to pull me out of that dream so I could go back to having real adventures!

HOW TO HELP THE DOCTOR DEFEAT THEM:

You and the Doctor are going to need each other if you run into these guys. You need to keep asking questions and working out if you're awake or asleep. If it seems too good to be true, then you're probably dreaming.

From: **Rose Tyler**
Subject: **TARDIS!!!!**
Date: **3 October 2005**
To: **Mickey Smith**

This is insane Mickey!!! I'm sending you an email on the TARDIS!!! I'm at the console now. One wrong button and I could send us flying into Jupiter or something . . .

DO NOT tell Mum I said that, she's so worried. But I'm safe. It's weird because I've never been in stranger and weirder places or seen things like this before, but I've never felt so safe as when I'm with the Doctor. I did feel scared of him at first. But I trust him more than anything now.

How are you? How's everything with – OH! Got to go, just landed somewhere that smells like onions!!! xo

From: **Mickey Smith**
Subject: **Where you at?**
Date: **29 September 2005**
To: **Rose Tyler**

Babe? Where you at? Message or email me yeah? Your mum is driving me mad. Just tell us you're OK and that there ain't no more aliens or anything coming. K?

MS x

From: **Rose Tyler**
Subject: **HELLO MUM!**
Date: **3 October 2005**
To: **Jackie Tyler**

Mum,
How are you? It's me! I told you I'd be in touch. Remember if you have any problems with your email then get Mickey round to help. **BUT DO NOT LET HIM READ THIS!**

MICKEY, IF YOU ARE READING THIS – GO AWAY, AND GIVE MUM SOME TIME!!!!

I've got so much to tell you. You won't believe what I've seen. Right now, I'm writing this on a planet, sipping something out of a great big blue alien pineapple thing! I've got my feet in something called dry water. It's like water, and you can swim in it, but you don't get wet. I can't explain it proper, but it's brilliant. It's fantastic!!!!!

I know he doesn't look alien. I mean, what kind of alien would have those ears? And yes, he does wear a lot of black, you're right about that. But that's his thing. You wouldn't expect to see him wearing bright trousers or a long, colourful scarf, would you? He's sad, you see. He lost his people in a great big space war and he's on his own. That's why he likes it when I'm there.

Got to run. Going to try something called lava-surfing!!!!

Love you, Rose xxxxxxx

DON'T LET HIM TRAVEL ALONE

You're with him now, and that's amazing. That's fantastic. And that's a lot of responsibility, so if you ever think about leaving him, make sure you really think it through – not just for yourself, but for his sake too. The Doctor shouldn't be alone. If you don't believe me, take a look at all the other people who've said it too.

CONVERSATIONS WITH THE DOCTOR

RIVER SONG

With Amy and Rory gone, the Doctor asked River to travel with him.

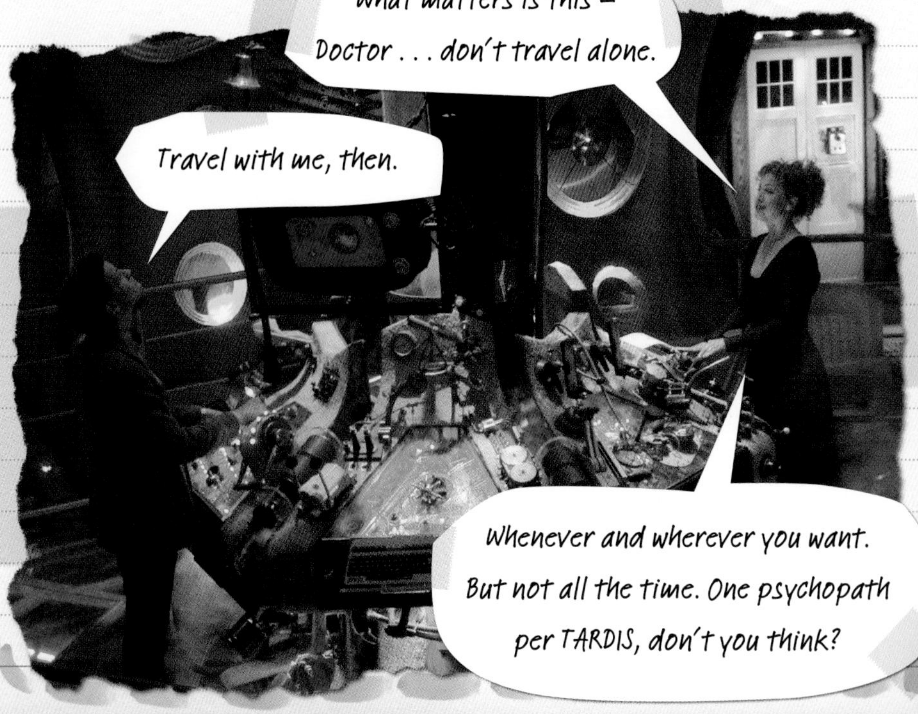

What matters is this – Doctor . . . don't travel alone.

Travel with me, then.

Whenever and wherever you want. But not all the time. One psychopath per TARDIS, don't you think?

AMY POND

Amy was zapped back in time, but left a message in a book for the Eleventh Doctor.

256

Afterword,
by Amelia Williams

Hello, old friend, and here we are.
You and me, on the last page. By the time you read these words, Rory and I will be long gone, so know that we lived well, and were very happy. And, above all else, know that we will love you, always. Sometimes I do worry about you though; I think, once we're gone, you won't be coming back here for a while, and you might be alone, which you should never be.

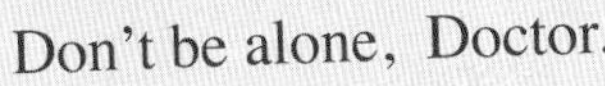

Don't be alone, Doctor.

ADELAIDE BROOKE

The Doctor saved Captain Adelaide Brooke and some of her crew from Mars. It was a fixed point in time, so he shouldn't have done it. If there is no one there to stop him, can he stop himself?

THE DOCTOR:

FOR A LONG TIME NOW, I THOUGHT I WAS JUST A SURVIVOR. BUT I'M NOT. I'M THE WINNER. THAT'S WHO I AM. THE TIME LORD VICTORIOUS.

ADELAIDE:

AND THERE'S NO ONE TO STOP YOU?

THE DOCTOR:

NO.

ADELAIDE:

THIS IS WRONG, DOCTOR. I DON'T CARE WHO YOU ARE. THE TIME LORD VICTORIOUS IS WRONG.

THE DOCTOR:

THAT'S FOR ME TO DECIDE.

When Amy, Rory and the Doctor faced a criminal in a funny old cowboy town called Mercy, the Doctor didn't want to help him. But, once again, Amy Pond was the voice of reason.

DONNA NOBLE

Donna Noble had a huge impact on the Doctor. A run-in with a fortune-teller and a Time Beetle showed her what the world would have been like had she never met the Doctor.

The fortune-teller created a parallel world where the Doctor and Donna never met because she turned right one day rather than left. That meant that when the Doctor battled the Empress of the Racnoss she wasn't there to tell him when to stop. The Doctor drowned below the Thames and this changed EVERYTHING!

A WORLD WITHOUT THE DOCTOR:

Without the Doctor, Martha Jones and Sarah Jane Smith would have given their lives to save everyone in the Royal Hope Hospital when the Judoon put it on the moon.

The Titanic starliner crashed to Earth, wiping out London!

Sixty million Americans were turned into Adipose!

The Torchwood team were lost when they saved Earth from being poisoned by the Sontarans. Captain Jack became trapped on Sontar!

TOP TEN REASONS WHY THE DOCTOR SHOULDN'T TRAVEL ALONE

1. He has more fun when there's someone to have fun with.
2. He needs you to remind him to be nice!
3. Playing I Spy on your own is no fun!
4. Someone has to tell him when to stop. He can get carried away.
5. He has better ideas when he can talk at you.
6. It's healthier because he has someone to share his crisps with.
7. He'll be a good man if you remind him of the rules.
8. He likes asking where you want to go and then taking you somewhere completely different.
9. It's twice as easy to explore when there are two of you.
10. It takes two to catch a monster – one to be bait and the other to set the trap! (I always seem to be the bait, now I think about it.)

NOT THE DOCTOR!

I'm telling you to put all of your trust in the Doctor . . . but I should probably make sure you're trusting the right Doctors!

THE META-CRISIS TENTH DOCTOR

Mix some leftover regeneration energy with the Doctor's spare hand and you'll get a human version of the Doctor. He has one heart and can age. Plus, he can't regenerate. A human Doctor – the perfect person to live a life with Rose Tyler.

NOW LIVES IN A PARALLEL UNIVERSE. WONDER IF HE'S STILL RUNNING . . .

GANGER ELEVENTH DOCTOR

While the Doctor was investigating the Flesh – a gross goo that made human doubles for tough jobs, called 'Gangers' – a solar storm hit the factory and made all o the Gangers believe they were human. The Doctor touche the Flesh and a Ganger version of the Doctor was create He turned out to be just like the Doctor and sacrificed himself to save everyone.

EVEN THOUGH HE WAS MADE FROM SLIME, HE WAS A PROPER DOCTO

GHOST TWELFTH DOCTOR

The Fisher King was a horrible alien who turned people into ghosts. He wanted them to transmit his coordinates so that his kind could pick up his body from a stasis chamber. When a ghostly version of the Doctor appeared, I thought that something terrible had happened to him. Turns out it was just a hologram created by the Doctor to trick everyone.

THIS IS ONE SERIOUSLY *CREEPY* GHOST!

SPOONHEAD ELEVENTH DOCTOR

Spoonheads were copies of people with hollow heads. They were robotic servers created by the Great Intelligence, and could suck people up into the Cloud as if they were online info. I know this because it happened to me. Twice! One of the Spoonheads looked like the Doctor, until he turned round and revealed his horrible head!

THE DOCTOR HACKED THIS ROBOT AND USED IT TO UPLOAD ITS OWN CONTROLLER TO THE CLOUD – CAUSING SOME REAL ISSUES FOR THEM. GOOD!

JACKSON LAKE

When this Victorian guy and his family were attacked by Cybermen, a Cyber infostamp projected loads of data into his head. This made him think he was the Doctor. He had a companion, a TARDIS (sort of) and a screwdriver (not sonic). The Tenth Doctor was pretty excited to meet him, but the truth was that he wasn't a Time Lord.

HE LOOKS LIKE HE COULD BE A DOCTOR, RIGHT?

MEGLOS FOURTH DOCTOR

This Zolfa-Thuran called Meglos trapped the Fourth Doctor and Romana in a time loop. He took the Doctor's form so that he could get his hands on the Dodecahedron, an artefact that powered a planet. He was basically a cactus – but extra prickly. Especially when the Fourth Doctor beat him.

NOT TO BE MIXED UP WITH A VINVOCCI (ALSO PRICKLY)!

TESELECTA ELEVENTH DOCTOR

When River Song blasted the Doctor, it wasn't actually the Doctor she killed – it was a shape-shifting time-travelling robot with a miniature crew inside, which looked like him. The Teselecta was a Justice Department vehicle that travelled through time and space, punishing bad guys. So River didn't kill anyone, but the universe thought the Doctor was gone!

CLARA OSWALD

Okay, so this might be a bit big-headed, but I've pretended to be the Doctor myself on quite a few occasions. So much so that one could say we're pretty similar in a few small ways. I'm not saying that you'll see me flying through time and space with my own TARDIS and companion or anything, but just remember I'm the Impossible Girl!

OSWALD FOR THE WIN!

WALKER GENERAL HOSPITAL

San Francisco

To Whom It May Concern,

The Seventh Doctor was brought in on 30 December 1999 with multiple gunshot wounds, and when I carried out exploratory surgery it caused complications that led to his regeneration. This was unfortunate, but in my defence, a binary vascular system isn't something you see every day – and I'm a heart doctor.

The Eighth Doctor convinced me he was the man I had failed to save, but he couldn't remember much else for a while. Then this awful man called the Master turned up, possessed me, killed me, tried to take the Doctor's lives and then fell into the Eye of Harmony. I was revived by the TARDIS. And here I am today. That's a long story made short – that forty-eight hours felt like a lifetime.

The Doctor was unlike anyone I had ever met before. He was so innocent and in awe of everything. He was wide-eyed and romantic. He said he was half human, but I think this was just his way of saying he could connect with humanity. He asked me to travel with him. I said no and asked him to stay with me. In the end we went our separate ways – but how do you forget someone like him?

Yours faithfully,

GHolloway

Dr Grace Holloway

ALL ABOUT ALIENS: ZYGONS

Zygons are shape-shifting aliens from space. They've got suckers and venomous sacs in their mouths . . . and they even have their own pet Loch Ness Monster!

WHAT ARE THEY?

These aliens have been known to kidnap humans and bodyprint them. That might sound arty, but it means keeping them prisoner so they can copy how they look and steal their identity. It happened to me. Not cool.

Sarah Jane Smith had a nasty scare when a rude Zygon interrupted her telephone call to the Doctor. She was used to trap him. The Zygons locked them both in a room without air – but the Doctor put them both in a trance so they didn't need to breathe!

The day the War Doctor, Tenth Doctor and Eleventh Doctor did what it took to stop the Time War, a Zygon invasion took place! Talk about bad timing. In the end, the Doctors confused UNIT and wiped the Zygons' memories – so that they couldn't remember which species they were on the side of – to force them to reach a peaceful conclusion.

A Zygon called Bonnie used my image to cause a lot of problems with UNIT. This Bonnie even tried to shoot the Doctor's plane down. She was dangerous all right, but, let's be honest, she looked great.

HOW TO HELP THE DOCTOR DEFEAT THEM:

Zygons keep developing – now they can create doubles using telepathy. This makes defeating them especially tricky. But when dealing with Zygons, always remember there are 20 million peaceful Zygons living on Earth – they're not all bad.

TARDIS TRAVEL ESSENTIALS!

I hope your bag is like the TARDIS. It'll need to be bigger on the inside to pack all of this away in it!

PART TWO

YO-YO

You might think that there's more to a yo-yo than a basic Earth toy, and you'd be right. The Doctor has used one for testing gravity on alien planets and confusing Vikings. Personally I find yo-yos useful for keeping busy when locked in alien prison cells! I'm getting quite good.

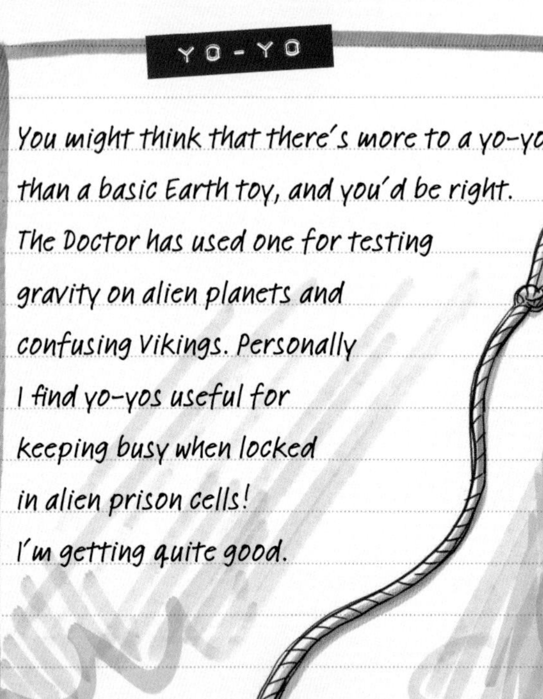

EMERGENCY UMBRELLA

I've been to places where it's basically rained for one thousand years straight, and I'm not just talking about Blackpool. So you'll need a big umbrella to keep you dry. If you're like the Seventh Doctor, and maybe you are, you can use an umbrella for fighting monsters and hanging off dangerous ledges.

A MAP

On occasion you might find yourself lost. Without the Doctor. Without the TARDIS. So make sure you've got a map. If you are lucky enough to find an alien species to give you a lift home, then they're going to need directions. Just be extra careful not to end up on Mondas, or any other planets that look like Earth, but aren't.

THE PATERNOSTER GANG'S RULES

How to deal with the Doctor, explained by the experts.

The Doctor is a wise man. You need to listen to him and take note, for what he says can end wars, save universes and turn lives around in an instant. Accept him for who and what he is and follow him. You will need loyalty and belief at all times. Only then will you be a true companion and worthy of a place at his side.

JENNY FLINT

What Ma'am says is right, you know. But I think there's more too. You've got to be ready for action and ready to run or fight at any moment. You'll need to follow him, as he's always in trouble – and he'll need your help getting him out of one sticky situation or another. Just because someone's wise, it don't mean they don't make silly mistakes. No offence, Ma'am.

COMMANDER STRAX

How would I deal with the Doctor? Easy! An underground attack with seventeen laser monkeys! This one's quite tall, so you may prefer to obtain a stepladder before you aim your personal rocket launcher at him . . .
How would I deal with being his companion? Do not be absurd, I am a Sontaran Commander. I do not serve others. Now, would you like some tea, or a refreshing glass of slime?

Hi, it's Ace here!

Here are the Professor's rules:

1. HE'S IN CHARGE.

Yeah! He is. You do what you're told when you're travelling with someone like him. After getting swept up in a time-storm and dropped on the other side of the universe I don't want to get stranded anywhere lame again. I also don't want to go home. I just want WICKED adventures!

He has this obsession with making me face my demons. He made me look back at all the things I'd done and all the things I had felt and got into my head. All of this was to train me up and make me a better person – something he's still doing. Maybe he thinks I'm going to be a Time Lord or something?

2. HE'S NOT THE PROFESSOR. HE'S THE DOCTOR.

Nah. Not to me. He's the PROFESSOR. Do I say it to wind him up? Maybe. But he teaches me stuff all the time, so that's more like a Professor than a Doctor, isn't it?

3. HE'LL MAKE UP THE REST OF THESE RULES BEFORE HE DROPS ME HOME IN PERIVALE.

We're going back to visit Perivale soon. And we still haven't made up any real rules. I mean, he wanted me to stop building my own explosives – but then he found my Nitro-9 pretty handy a few times for blowing up Cybermen and Daleks. I did respect his wishes, though, and didn't blow EVERYTHING up. Sometimes I used my baseball bat instead.

Anyway, I don't know who you are or why you want this, but here you go. Hope it helps you and the Professor!

MOST WANTED (PART TWO)

You thought there'd only be two pages of alien nasties to look out for? Think again. And then never stop thinking . . .

Skovox Blitzer

These robots were built for war. Anything built for war is never going to be good. They have powerful scuttling legs and are armed to the back teeth with mega-lasers. (I don't know if they actually have back teeth, or any teeth – they probably don't need them.) One of these robots can destroy a planet, so get them OFF the planet as soon as possible.

The Teller

Who knows what this species is really called, or where they're from, but they have some seriously scary skills. One was used as a guard in the Bank of Karabraxos – it could telepathically sense guilt in people planning bad things. Then it would liquefy their brains.

The Graske

Not met one of these little fellas, but I've heard some pretty bad things about the Graske. They can shape-shift, they carry out work for the Trickster and they're very annoying, apparently. Not to be confused with Groske, who are small, blue and also annoying, but they're the good guys.

Clockwork Droids

The Tenth Doctor and Rose had a run-in with these creepy robots in 51st-century space and 18th-century Paris. The Doctor called them rubbish robots from the dawn of time. They were always repairing themselves with human body parts – nasty.

Snowmen

Brrrrrr. These things properly give me the chills. Maybe because one of the other versions of me had a pretty bad time with them. Controlled by the Great Intelligence, these frosty freaks had icy fangs and an appetite for humans.

MONSTER WATCH!

Quick test! I warned you, I am a teacher. Now let's see if you've got what it takes to spot aliens in disguise.

Question 1

You notice that everyone in your class stops moving if you hold your breath, so . . .

a) you give them a weird stare.

b) you run off as quickly as possible.

c) you keep holding it, because you're surrounded by Clockwork Droids!

Question 2

You spot a large, trumpy person with a zip on their forehead. What do you think?

a) Nothing, it's probably just a fashion thing.

b) How strange, I'd better look into this . . .

c) That's a Slitheen in disguise. Get me some vinegar!

Question 3

Your friend is acting weird and looks a bit shiny, so you decide that they're . . .

a) wearing a lot of sun cream. It's the sensible thing to do in summer!

b) auditioning for the school play, for the part of Shop Dummy Number One.

c) an Auton. That's plastic controlled by the Nestene Consciousness. You need some anti-plastic, and quick!

Question 4

Your teacher is behaving oddly and has big red suckers popping up on their skin. This means only one thing!

a) Yeah, it means it's term time.

b) Octopus invasion!

c) Your teacher is a Zygon clone. Get the Doctor – the peace treaty may be under threat!

HOW DID YOU ANSWER?

Mostly As
Monster mistake!
Hmmmm. You need to start asking more questions and spotting the clues. Aliens are all around you, but you're not seeing them!

Mostly Bs
Monster mind!
You know weird things are going on, and you know about monsters and aliens – but you're not taking action!

Mostly Cs
Monster master!
You know all of the signs for spotting aliens disguised as humans. You're super sharp, sorted and ready to run!

WHICH COMPANION ARE YOU MOST LIKE?

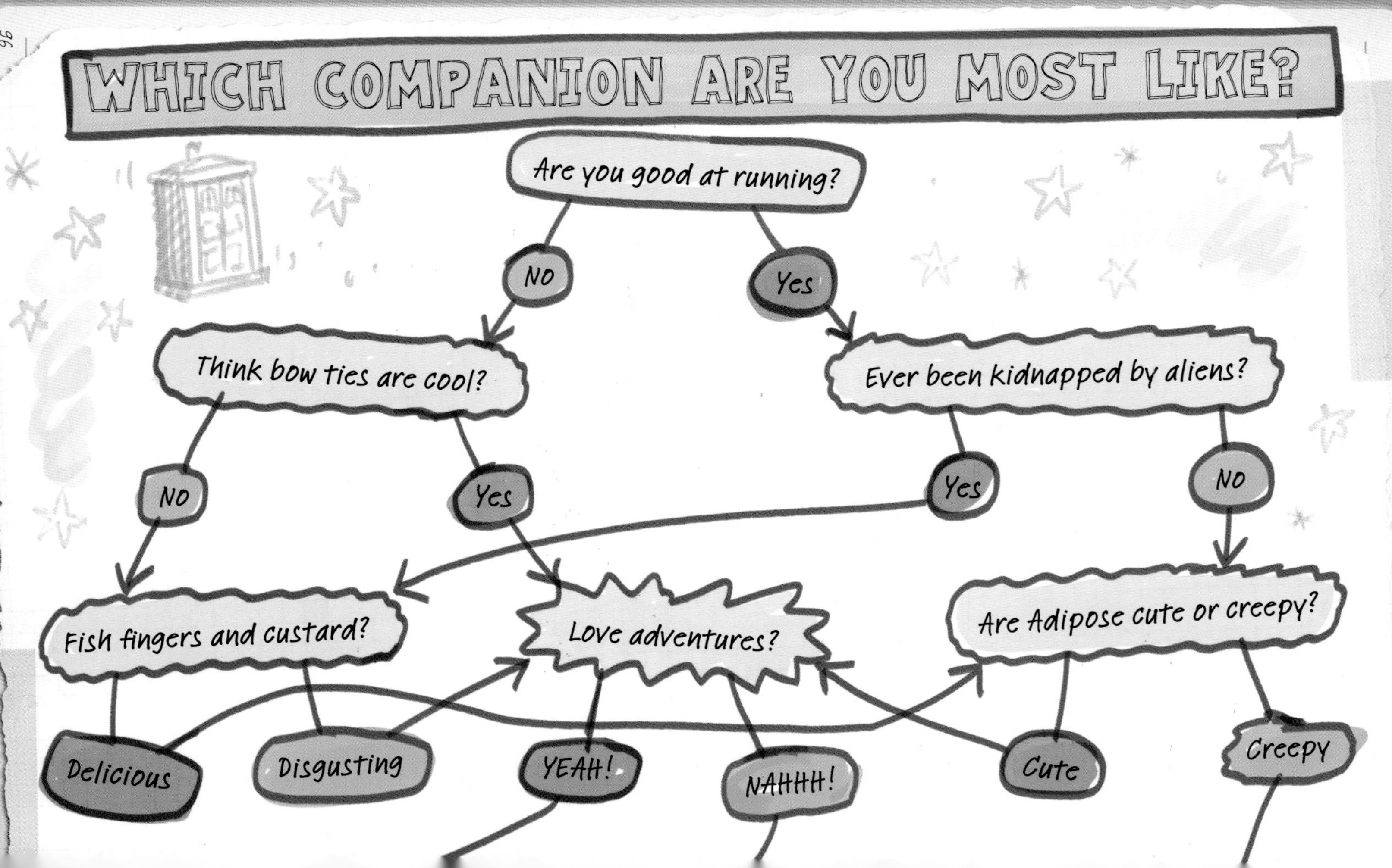

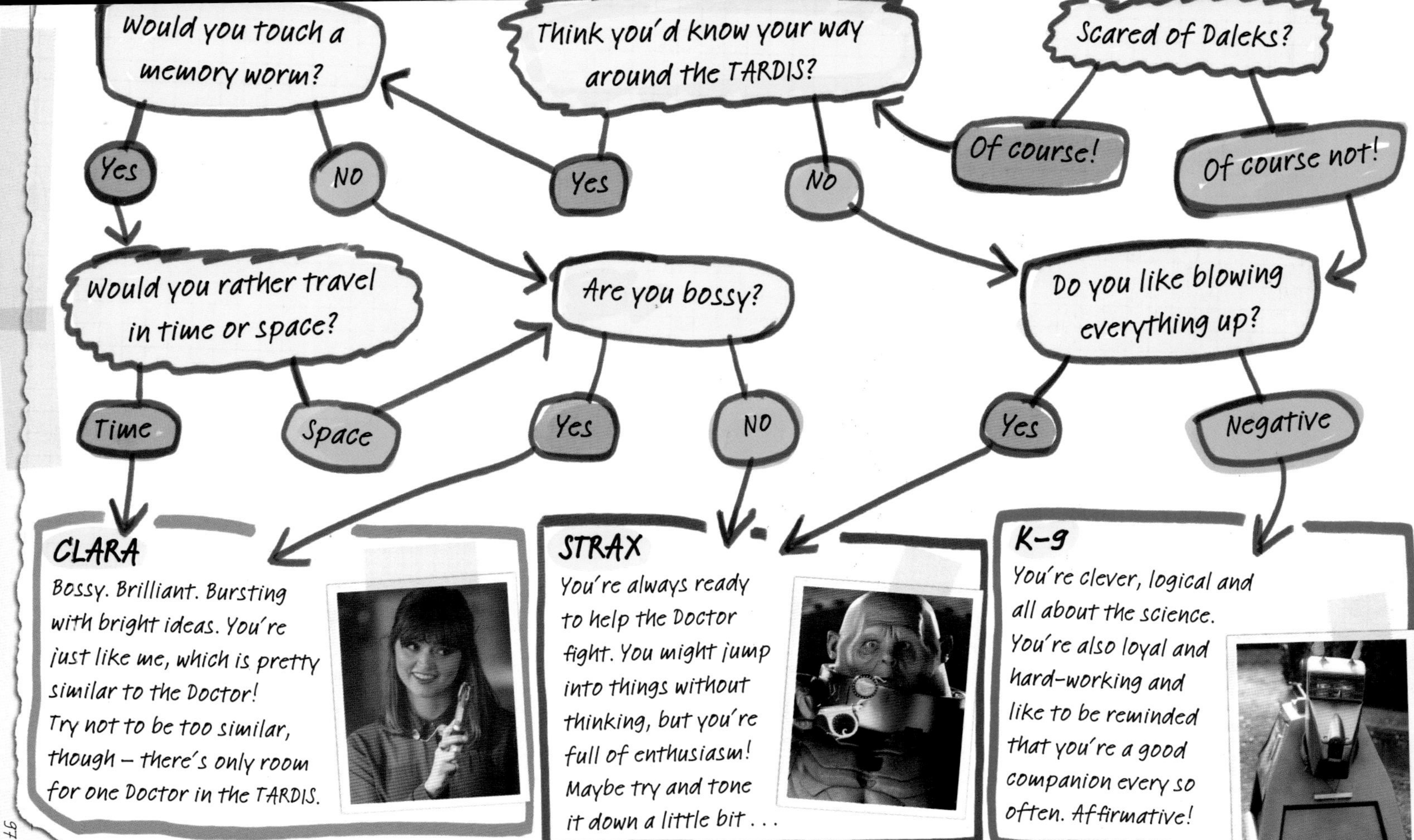

Would you touch a memory worm?
Yes
NO
Think you'd know your way around the TARDIS?
Yes
NO
Scared of Daleks?
Of course!
Of course not!
Would you rather travel in time or space?
Time
Space
Are you bossy?
Yes
NO
Do you like blowing everything up?
Yes
Negative
CLARA
Bossy. Brilliant. Bursting with bright ideas. You're just like me, which is pretty similar to the Doctor! Try not to be too similar, though – there's only room for one Doctor in the TARDIS.
STRAX
You're always ready to help the Doctor fight. You might jump into things without thinking, but you're full of enthusiasm! Maybe try and tone it down a little bit . . .
K-9
You're clever, logical and all about the science. You're also loyal and hard-working and like to be reminded that you're a good companion every so often. Affirmative!

WHAT'S YOUR SONIC?

Take this test to see which sonic would suit you!

WHAT TO DO:

Choose the five words that you like best. Then see if you've chosen one colour the most – if not, keep choosing words until it's clear which colour suits you!

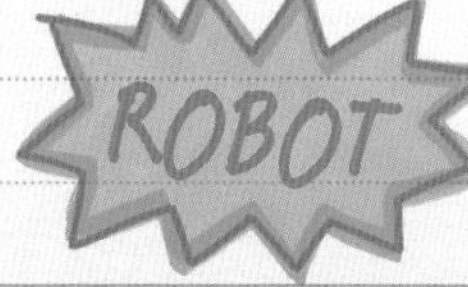

PURPLE – sonic shades

Just like the Twelfth Doctor, you like to be cool and clever. These sunglasses are packed with tech and will definitely suit you – you scan what you want, when you want and no one will know!

BLUE – sonic screwdriver

This is the sonic of choice for most of the Doctors and perfect for when you want to get the job done. Send for help, summon the TARDIS or blow up a few robots with this handy handheld device!

GREEN – sonic cane

Wow! You're pretty sophisticated – perhaps you like wearing bow ties and top hats too? That's good news, because a certain someone I travelled with thinks they're cool. This is your basic sonic – but helps you walk fancy.

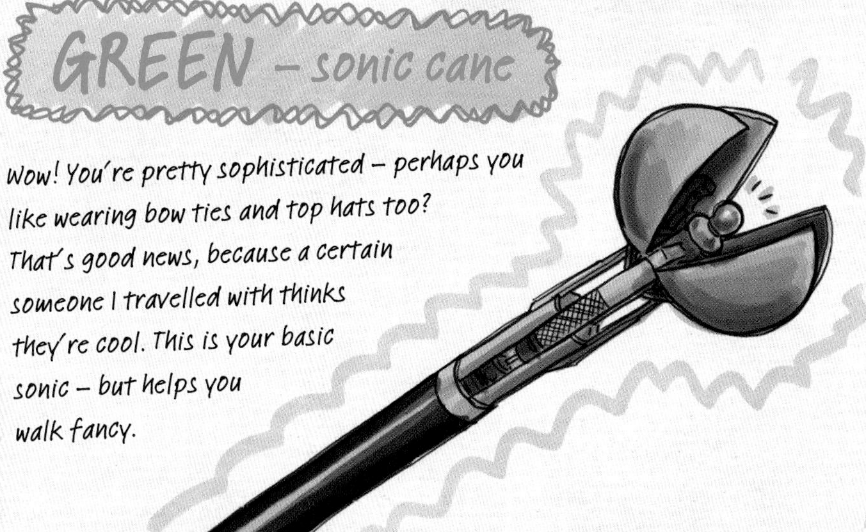

RORY'S WEIRDEST MOMENTS

Hello, this is Rory Pond . . . Williams! Rory Williams, I mean! I travelled with the Doctor and my wife, Amy, and some pretty weird stuff happened. UNIT asked me to put a few notes together, so here they are.

And they're all true.

Yes. Enjoy.

Right. So I was wiped from existence because I was sucked into a crack in time. BOO! But then I came back as a Roman soldier. YAY! Turns out I was an Auton made out of plastic, though. I then ended up guarding Amy in the Pandorica for nearly 2,000 years. I'm back to normal now.

Fish from space. Yeah. Weird. They were all over Venice with their smelly fish breath and pointy teeth – and I had to have a scrap with one to protect the woman I love. I won, of course. Amy only helped about 75%.

When Amy was kidnapped, the Doctor and I went on the rampage. I had to send a message to the Cybermen so they knew I was serious – so I blew up their entire Cyber Fleet. Not bad for someone who gets nervous visiting the hairdresser's.

I had a ponytail! It was just a dream one. Or a nightmare one. Depends how you feel about men with ponytails.

The Doctor popped out of a cake at my stag do! How many people can say that? Sadly, probably quite a few.

Oh yeah, and I've died loads and come back loads. I've been:

- Blasted by a Silurian heat ray.
- Turned to dust by an Eknodine in a dream world.
- Drowned in the sea, thanks to a Siren and some pirates.
- Aged to death in the TARDIS by an angry asteroid.

POSTCARDS FROM PERI

POST CARD

Hey guys,

Still travelling with the Doctor, but he's not the same man I met on Lanzarote. We visited Androzani Minor and became very ill. There was only enough antidote for one – and he gave it to me. He didn't die but he became a whole new person. He was so quiet and soft before, but now he's loud and a bit cuckoo. I don't know if I can trust him yet – he said it's going take some time to adjust. Fingers crossed, right?

Peri ♡

Hey,
Back on Earth – but not for long! The Cybermen had a plan to destroy this planet – using Halley's comet! Can you believe it? They also wanted to use time travel to bring back their home planet, Mondas. The Doctor put a stop to that. He's not so different from the other guy, in a way. It's hard to explain.
Peri
WISH YOU WERE HERE!
I.M. FOREMAN, 76 TOTTER'S LANE.
POST
Me again!
So this time I end up in an adventure with not just one Time Lord, but two Time Lords and a Time Lady! The Doctor loves to lecture – and you know how much I hate to be lectured. But he is a hero. The Master and the Rani – the Time Lord and Time Lady I mentioned – are power mad. The Doctor sent the Rani's TARDIS flying out of the universe – and the Rani and the Master were trapped in it, with a T. rex. I am not kidding.
Peri

TIME WITH K-9

If you want to know about being a companion, then you've got to talk to all of them. Even the robot dog ones.

Hello, K-9.

Greetings, Mistress Clara Oswald.

How are you?

All components are functioning normally.

That means you're well?

Affirmative, Mistress.

When did you first meet the Doctor?

I am K-9 Mark IV. The Doctor encountered K-9 Mark I after Professor Marius built it in the year 5000 on the asteroid K4067. I share the knowledge and data collected by my previous versions.

Did you meet any of the Doctor's companions?

Affirmative. Mistress Leela, Mistress Romana, Mistress Sarah Jane Smith and Mistress Rose Tyler.

Additionally, I encountered Mickey Smith, who incorrectly referred to himself as a 'tin dog'.

Who was your favourite?

I regarded them all as unpredictable organic life forms, Mistress. May I enquire as to why you ask? Do you wish to be associated with the title of 'most successful companion'?

No. Shut up. Forget it.

Erasing memory . . .

No, I didn't mean . . .

Memory successfully erased.

. . . Oh, well, all right then. What advice do you have for travelling with the Doctor?

Always remain vigilant, logical and loyal. Intelligence and accuracy are highly valued assets.

What else would be helpful?

Lasers and a teleport function would be most helpful.

Can you bark?

I am not programmed to bark.

This hasn't been very helpful, K-9.

I regret that I was not able to advance your studies in this matter, Mistress. I recommend questions of further depth and detail next time.

Are you being a bad dog on purpose?

Affirmative.

KEEP THE DOCTOR AWAY FROM . . .

Here are six things you HAVE TO keep out of the Doctor's way!

1. THE PANDORICA

This is a trap made especially for the Doctor. All of the aliens in the universe got together to put him in it! If you see anything like it, then you need to get him out of there. It's a real pain to spend 2,000 years in.

2. MEMORY WORMS

Touch one of these wiggly fellas and you lose your short-term memory. If the Doctor has one on purpose it means he's up to something very, very tricky. If he has one by accident, you'll have a couple of very, very tricky hours with the Doctor.

3. CUSTARD

Okay, so this isn't quite so dramatic, but give the Doctor a bowl of custard and he'll just find weird things to dip in it. Avoid.

4. TIME LORDS

Tough, this one, because for a long time he believed he was the last of them. He was so lonely and so sad. But when Time Lords turn up, it always means trouble for the Doctor.

5. BABIES

He likes babies. Who doesn't like babies? The problem is, the Doctor can talk baby, and that usually means that he translates something embarrassing. When a baby is too honest it gets AWKWARD!

6. THE MOMENT

More Time Lord tech. This one is a weapon. You know how the Doctor feels about weapons. And this weapon might be one of the worst of all time. If you see this, feel free to go and get some custard, babies and memory worms to use as distractions.

ALL ABOUT ALIENS:

ICE WARRIORS

Keep your cool around these ancient warriors . . .

WHAT ARE THEY?

They're Martians – as in, they're aliens from Mars. They're basically strong lizards inside bio-armour. This armour is tough and advanced and can even walk around on its own without an Ice Warrior in it. They are ancient, clever and honourable.

Victoria was chased through glacier caves by a nasty Ice Warrior called Turoc. She's probably the only person in the world who was pleased to have an avalanche fall on top of her. It stopped Turoc and gave her the chance to cry for help.

The Third Doctor and Jo visited the planet Peladon as it tried to join this Galactic Federation thing. All sorts of weird stuff happened, and everyone thought it was the Ice Warriors' doing, but it wasn't! The coolest thing was that the Doctor introduced Jo as Princess Josephine of TARDIS, and everyone called her that!

I thought I was going to Vegas with the Eleventh Doctor but we ended up on a Russian submarine in the 1980s . . . with an Ice Warrior on board. It was found in a block of ice, but escaped and went after everyone, including me. In the end, though, the Ice Warrior stopped the weapons going off – which is a big deal for a species all about the fighting.

HOW TO HELP THE DOCTOR DEFEAT THEM:

Ice Warriors can be reasoned with . . . so let the Doctor talk to them. And, if that doesn't work, you should talk to them. Yes, you! Be honest, be brave and be understanding. Then be ready to run if that doesn't work out.

YES OR NO!

DOCTOR SAID NO

The Doctor doesn't always get what he wants. Some people have said no to travelling with him – and sometimes he's said no to them.

ADAM MITCHELL

This guy had one journey with the Ninth Doctor and Rose, but ruined it by getting a weird alien-brain implant and trying to use future tech to his own advantage. Click your fingers around him to open a window in his forehead. It's quite good fun.

JOURNEY BLUE

This soldier travelled inside a Dalek with me and the Doctor. She tried to come away with us afterwards, but the Doctor's not a fan of soldiers.

CAPTAIN JACK

He's a hero and he's had plenty of adventures with the Doctor but, because he was made immortal by the power of the Time Vortex, he became a fixed point in time. That means he really messes with the TARDIS.

DECLINED

THEY SAID NO

PERKINS

APPROVED

The Chief Engineer on the Orient Express worked pretty well with the Doctor when investigating mysterious mummy attacks. The Doctor asked him to stay on the TARDIS, but Perkins declined. He said 'that job could change a man'.

OSGOOD

Petronella Osgood might have been a huge fan of the Doctor, but he was also a pretty big fan of hers. He asked her to join us for an adventure, but sadly Missy got there first. Then the two Osgoods chose to stay on Earth and look after the planet.

APPROVED

GRACE HOLLOWAY

She helped the Eighth Doctor after he went through a tricky regeneration – and she helped beat the Master. But Grace didn't want to travel with the Doctor. She had her own life and her own plans.

APPROVED

WHO CAN HELP? PART 2:

DORIUM MALDOVAR AND CAPTAIN JACK

So one's now a head in a box and the other is apparently a face in a jar – but these guys are full of helpful info.

DORIUM MALDOVAR

WHO IS HE?

Dorium owned the Maldovarium bar in the 52nd century. He did a few dodgy dealings and knew a few dangerous characters. Dorium was beheaded by the Headless Monks while helping save Amy at Demon's Run. His head now lives on in the Seventh Transept.

HOW CAN HE HELP?

His head may no longer be connected to his body, but Dorium is a well-connected man. He knows all about aliens, rumours, myths and the Doctor. He also has a chip in his head that picks up Wi-Fi!

LET HIM:

- Tell you everything he knows.
- Do a few deals to get you what you want.

DON'T LET HIM:

- Trick you with riddles.
- Sell you anything.

CAPTAIN JACK

WHO IS HE?

Captain Jack Harkness (not his real name) is a Time Agent from the 51st century. He was exterminated by Daleks, but when Rose Tyler was Bad Wolf she brought him back to life . . . forever. Jack went back in time and headed up Torchwood.

HOW CAN HE HELP?

He'll fight for the Doctor, for you – and for Earth. He's used to aliens and dangerous situations and dying. The Doctor's warned me that he can be all smiles and teeth, and he's made some bad choices. But when you need a friend he'll be there.

LET HIM:

- Give you info on aliens.
- Be an action hero.

DON'T LET HIM:

- Get Torchwood involved.
- Be exterminated again.

FRIENDS AND FAMILY

If you enter the Doctor's world, then there is a good chance he's going to enter yours. You should warn him about your friends and family . . . and warn them about him too!

JACKIE TYLER

Rose's mum wasn't happy about the Doctor taking her daughter off. She showed her concern by giving him a right old slap. But after getting involved in the Battle of Canary Wharf she finally understood the Doctor.

FRANCINE JONES

Martha's mum never warmed to the Doctor. She and her family did have a tough time at the hands of the Master. (She also gave the Doctor a slap, by the way!)

SYLVIA NOBLE

Donna's mum never slapped the Doctor, but she did give him a big telling-off. But then he gave her a telling-off for not being nicer to Donna. That kept her quiet for a few minutes.

GOOD GRANDPARENTS

WILFRED MOTT

Donna's grandad made a huge impact on the Doctor. In the end the Doctor gave up his life to save Wilf.

MY GRAN

My gran was rather amused by the Eleventh Doctor. But then he did turn up to Christmas dinner naked.

BRILL BOYFRIENDS

MICKEY SMITH

Poor old Mickey Smith. The Doctor thought he was pretty useless. And so did Rose. And so did Jackie. But he got braver and more confident and ended up fighting Cybermen in a parallel universe!

RORY WILLIAMS

Because Amy had always grown up talking about her Raggedy Man, Rory felt very much second place. But Amy could never forget Rory Williams from Leadworth. She'd do anything for him.

DANNY PINK

How can I even write about Danny? The Doctor wrote him off, but he was a true hero. When I lost him and he came back as a Cyberman, he took control of the Cyber Army and saved us by leading them all to self-destruct.

ALL THE DOCTORS!

I visited Trenzalore. I visited the Doctor's grave. I entered the Doctor's time stream and broke into a million pieces and lived a million lives – all to help the Doctor. I've been a companion more times than anyone else in existence.

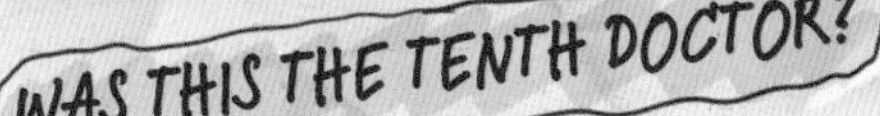

SNAZZY OUTFIT.

LOOK AT HIM GO!

OH, THIS FACE IS ONE OF MY FAVES!

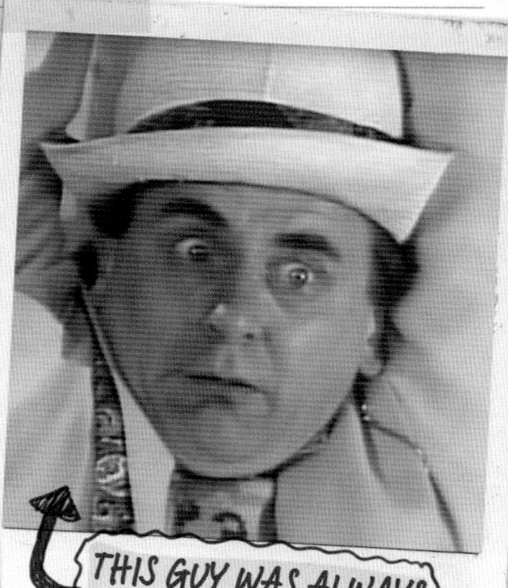
THIS GUY WAS ALWAYS HANGING AROUND . . .

OH, DEAR – IN TROUBLE AGAIN!

I TOLD HIM WHICH TARDIS TO TAKE.
YOU'RE WELCOME, DOCTOR!

HOW TO WIN!

Commander Strax here! Want to know the best way to serve your twig-like Doctor? Then see below!

DILEMMA 1

Dalek Strike!

Blow them up. Impress your clone batch by releasing an assortment of blast-weasels on the Dalek enemy. Three per Dalek should suffice. The sprightly little fellows go straight for the eyestalk!

DILEMMA 2

Cyber Invasion!

Blow them up. These inferior mechanoids are not worthy of existence, so put them out of their rusty misery by showering them with electric grenades. I recommend shouting 'surprise' if light humour is your thing.

DILEMMA 3

JUDOON PLATOON!

Blow them up, of course! Honour the Sontaran Empire, or whichever Empire you serve, by disintegrating these ridiculous rhinos. Obliterate them with supercharged thermos magnets or try dropping a piano on them. Sontar, ha!

DILEMMA 4

SONTARAN SLAM!

Blow them up? Do not be ridiculous. The glorious Sontaran Empire cannot simply be blown up. That said, we are a magnificent collection of the finest warrior soldiers in the galaxy and so we demand the courtesy of your attempts at our destruction! However, you will fail.

P.S. Do not tell General Staal that I said this, but an ideal solution to an impending Sontaran menace is to blow them up.

HOW TO HUNT GHOSTS!

Do ghosts really exist? The Doctor isn't convinced, but that hasn't stopped us trying to catch them!

FINDING GHOSTS

Learn about haunted locations rich with history. It's not just castles and old houses that are haunted. It could be schools or shoe shops.

HORRIFIC HAUNTING?

Look for the signs of a haunting, such as flickering lights, strange whispers and dro in temperature. You should keep an eye out for goo too. Mostly because it's nasty.

DON'T GO ALONE!

Why go somewhere spooky alone? You need friends to keep you going. That's what's so brilliant about being with the Doctor – sometimes you'll need to be there to hold him back, and other times you'll need him there to push you forward!

NOT GHOSTS!

They're spooky . . . but they're just not ghosts!

THE CALIBURN GHAST

This one was actually just a time-traveller called Hila Tacorien. She got trapped in a pocket universe which projected strange ghostly images into this world. The Doctor and I rescued her and sorted it!

THE GELTH

The Gelth were aliens whose bodies were reduced to gas in the Time War. They wanted a physical form, so they took over dead human bodies! Gross!

CYBERMEN

Once Rose and the Tenth Doctor returned to London to find that everyone thought the ghosts of their loved ones had appeared. But those weird shapes were actually Cybermen punching through from another universe!

THE FISHER KING'S SIGNALS

The Doctor and I thought we'd met actual, real, proper ghosts, but they were created by an alien called the Fisher King who turned people into ghostlike signals to his friends. The Doctor created his own ghost from a hologram to help stop it!

ALL ABOUT ALIENS: WEEPING ANGELS

They might look like statues, but if you turn your back, or close your eyes, or even blink . . . they'll zap you back in time.

WHAT ARE THEY?

The Weeping Angels are also known as the Lonely Assassins. They're quantum locked, which means they can't move if someone's looking at them. One touch from them sends you back in time – and they feed off the energy from the life you would have lived.

Martha Jones and the Doctor were sent back in time by Weeping Angels. Luckily for both of them, Sally Sparrow came to the rescue after they left a weird message for her in her favourite films.

Talk about a nightmare scenario – Amy Pond had to walk through a forest of Weeping Angels when she couldn't see. The Doctor guided her, but still, I wouldn't fancy that very much.

After dealing with a hotel packed with Weeping Angels, Amy and Rory faced the Statue of Liberty! They created a temporal paradox that stopped the angels, but one survived and blasted Rory into the 1930s. Amy followed him there.

HOW TO HELP THE DOCTOR DEFEAT THEM:

Just . . . just don't get zapped back in time. He doesn't handle that well. He doesn't like goodbyes and that's what these monsters specialise in. If you can't find a crack in time to send the Weeping Angels into, then set them up to look at each other so they're quantum locked forever! Mirrors work well for this.

LIFE AFTER THE DOCTOR

By Sarah Jane Smith

What's life like after having so many amazing adventures? Well, who's to say the adventures have to stop?

Never stop exploring! Never stop investigating. I've been an investigative journalist for years and years. Asking questions and not giving up until you find the answers takes you to amazing places. You'll also meet friends old and new, who, like you, can't resist a mystery.

Being on one planet for so long isn't such a bad thing. It gives you time to build a life around you. You might be a part of a family, or create your own family with friends you trust above all else.

You never know when adventure will call. You always have to be ready to run and join in – because if that blue box appears, you will definitely want to get back in it. Nothing beats helping the Doctor and his friends to stop alien bullies and save the world.

You might think you won't see the Doctor again. You might think you've been forgotten. Or replaced. But it's not like that – it's never like that. You're a part of him and his life and the lives of all the other companions.

I've seen amazing things out there in space, but strange things can happen wherever you are. You just need to know where to look. I have learned that life on Earth can be an adventure too.

THE NAME OF THE DOCTOR

He's had many lives and many names – some he chooses, some he's given. It's pretty handy for you to know what they all are, just in case he surprises you with one.

- Sir Doctor of TARDIS
- The President of Earth
- Raggedy Man
- Sherlock Holmes
- Professor
- John Smith
- Captain Grumpy
- The Valeyard
- Damsel
- Doctor Mysterio
- The Traveller From Beyond Time
- John Disco
- Old One
- Doctor James McCrimmon
- The Caretaker
- Basil
- Predator of the Daleks
- The Eyebrows
- The Great Exterminator
- The Architect
- Captain Troy Handsome
- Merlin

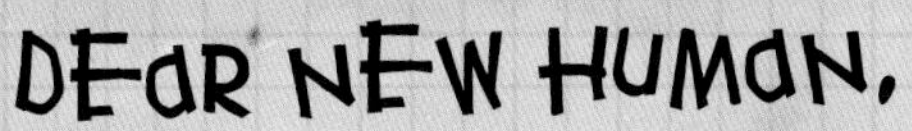

COMMANDER STRAX HERE AGAIN. THE BOY CALLED CLARA WHO HAS WRITTEN THIS GUIDE FOR YOU HAS PROBABLY MISSED OUT THE FOLLOWING:

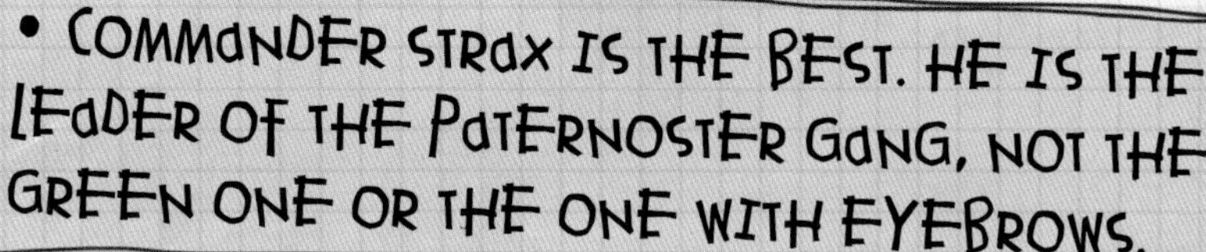

• SONTARANS ARE GLORIOUS. WORSHIP THE EMPIRE.

SONTAR, HA!

GIVE STRAX ALL THE SWEETS THAT YOU FIND.

• CARRY A MEMORY WORM AT ALL TIMES.

WHAT AM I DOING HERE?

WHAT IS THIS LIST?

WHERE AM I?

AN INTERVIEW WITH TEGAN

Transcript of interview with the Doctor's companion, Tegan Jovanka.

PRESENT:
Tegan Jovanka
UNIT Officer: P. White

UNIT OFFICER WHITE: Please introduce yourself.

TEGAN JOVANKA: I'm Tegan Jovanka and you've asked me here to talk about my time with the Doctor.

UNIT OFFICER WHITE: When did you first meet the Doctor?

TEGAN: I was driving to the first day of my new job as an air stewardess and BLAM, I only go and get a flat tyre, don't I?! I need help with my punctured tyre, see a blue police box and think 'Great, I'll get the cops to help'. Anyhow, I meet the Doctor and Adric. Adric was this little guy who was really into maths. The Doctor is, like, this big guy who invented maths. Super clever. Sorry, you have to tell me if I'm being too gobby. My aunty always said I haven't got my head screwed on! Really . . .

UNIT OFFICER WHITE: Please tell us about the fifth incarnation of the Doctor.

TEGAN: Oh yes! I saw him change. The Fourth Doctor had huge hair and this big voice. Then he became someone completely different. The Fifth

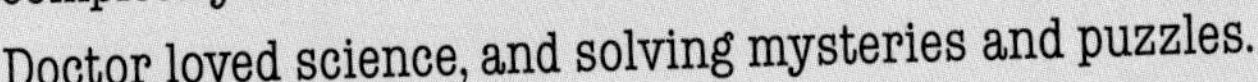

Doctor loved science, and solving mysteries and puzzles. He wore celery on his jacket. He was always thinking and sometimes he shared his thoughts and sometimes he didn't and –

UNIT OFFICER WHITE: You chose to stop travelling with the Doctor. Why?

TEGAN: We lost Adric, and I took that kinda hard, and after having dealt with the Mara – twice – and then the Daleks, I thought it was time to go. It just stopped being fun. And as my aunty said to me and I said to the Doctor, 'If you stop enjoying it, then give it up.'

UNIT OFFICER WHITE: Let's continue with the interview.

TEGAN: Nah, I'm not enjoying it, so I'm giving it up. I've got to get back to Heathrow.

ALIEN FIRST AID

Compiled by Dr Martha Jones

Travelling with the Doctor doesn't always mean fighting aliens – some of them need help. And sometimes it takes more than one Doctor.

HERE ARE MY TOP TIPS FOR TREATING COMMON ALIEN AILMENTS.

JUDOON HORN ROT

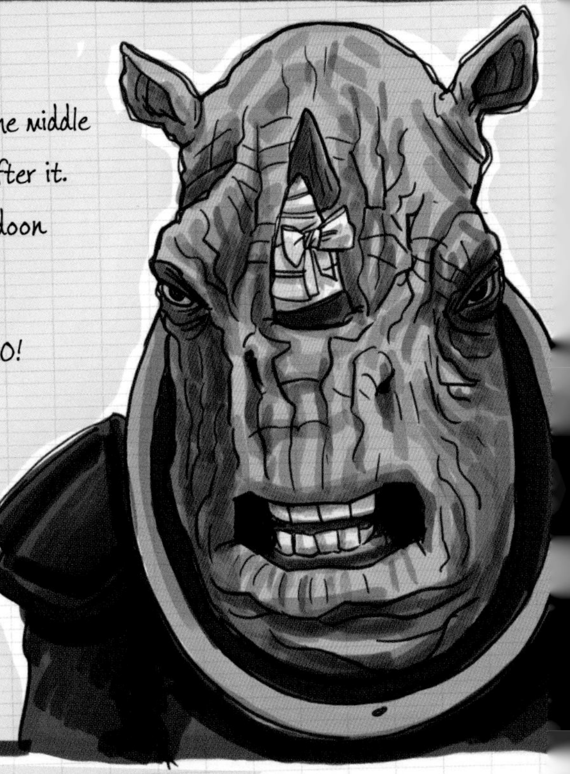

If you've got a big rhino horn in the middle of your mush, you need to look after it. Judoon horn rot occurs when Judoon wear their helmets for too long.

TREATMENT: BO! FRO! SKO!

Go without your helmet for two to three weeks and keep the horn dry. Poor Judoon, it almost makes you understand why they're so stampy all the time.

SILURIAN TONGUE TWIST

Silurians have long poisonous tongues to strike their victims with. Occasionally they can get themselves in a total tangle and end up with their tongue in a knot. Knot a pretty sight!

TREATMENT: You'll need thick gloves and lots of patience. Use your hands to untangle the tongue trouble, staying well back. Tell them: no flies for twenty-four hours.

LEONIAN FURBALLS

Okay, so this job might seem more suited to a vet, but Leonians are actually humanoids. These part-human, part-cat creatures still suffer from the number-one cat problem, though: coughing up furballs!

TREATMENT: Easy, this one. Tell them to stop licking themselves. Furballs are harmless, but they're pretty disgusting to see regurgitated.

TOP TIPS:

1. Make sure you're safe before helping others.
2. Keep patients awake and ask if they're okay.
3. GET HELP. Preferably from a doctor . . . or the Doctor.
4. REMEMBER: no matter how strange or weird an alien looks, they might be scared and in pain – so be kind.
5. WEAR AN APRON. Sometimes there can be a lot of slime. Actually, in my experience, not just sometimes – ALL the time.

THE FOURTH DOCTOR

By Sarah Jane Smith

Very different from the Third Doctor

Ruffles became hats

This Doctor uses 'reverse psychology' and is happy to tell you one thing to make you do another. It's annoying. It seems to work.

Capes became scarves

Bessie became TARDIS

He tried to talk to Davros during the birth of the Daleks – he wanted to stop the creatures from existing, but he couldn't wipe them out from existence forever. Even though we know what they become – is this right or wrong????

He returned to Gallifrey and had to go alone. He dropped me off in ~~South Croydon~~ Aberdeen! I told him not to forget me! I have a feeling I will see him again.

There's no point being grown up if you can't be childish sometimes!

Big fan of jelly babies – do Time Lords **NEED** sugar?

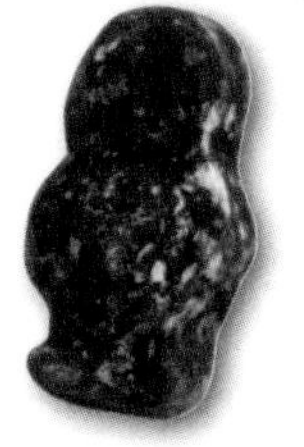

Together we've faced:

- A giant robot
- Wirrn
- Sontarans (Field Major Styre)
- Daleks
- Davros
- Thals
- Zygons
- Cybermen
- Anti-matter creature
- Sutekh
- Kraals
- Morbius
- Krynoids
- Mandragora Helix
- Eldrad

TARDIS TRAVEL ESSENTIALS!

Like I said before – you're going to need a bigger bag. Especially for these last-minute travel must-haves!

EARPLUGS

Sometimes you'll find yourself needing a good night's sleep and earplugs might just do the job. Plug them in and enjoy the silence.

(Note: not THE SILENCE)

Other times you might find them useful when the Doctor won't stop waffling on about something geniusly genius that he just wants to genius on about.

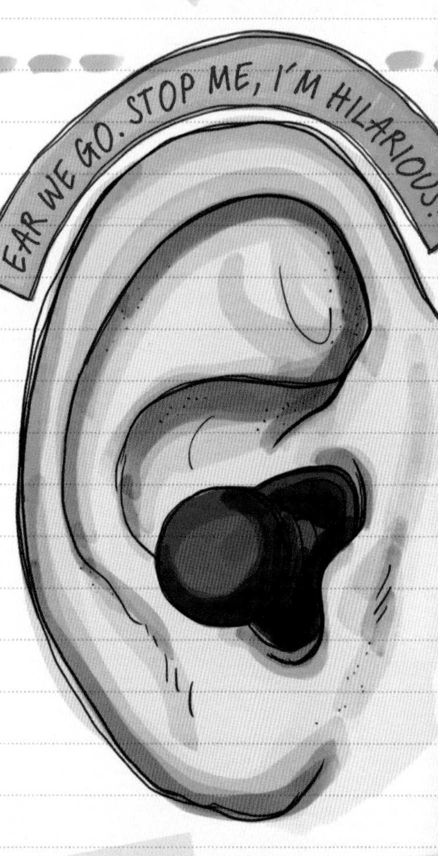

EXTRA:

Earplugs are also very handy for blocking out Sirens or any other creatures that like to lull you in, send you to sleep or screech on about stuff.

VORTEX MANIPULATOR

You've got the TARDIS, and the TARDIS is amazing, but if you need to travel through time quickly and easily with a great big headache, then get your hands on a Time Agency Vortex Manipulator.

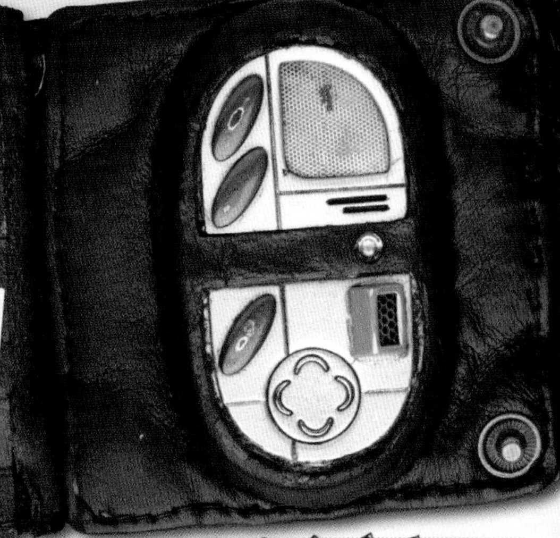

US COMPANIONS HAVE THE HABIT OF FINDING THEM, AND THEY'RE PRETTY USEFUL.

MEAT

I'm not saying that you SHOULD carry a pork chop around in your bag. I'm just saying that some aliens MIGHT love devouring huge pieces of meat, so you COULD carry a pork chop around in your bag. One of those things that isn't a great idea until it becomes a great idea.

BAD FOR: vegetarians.

PERFECT FOR: quick escapes and distractions.

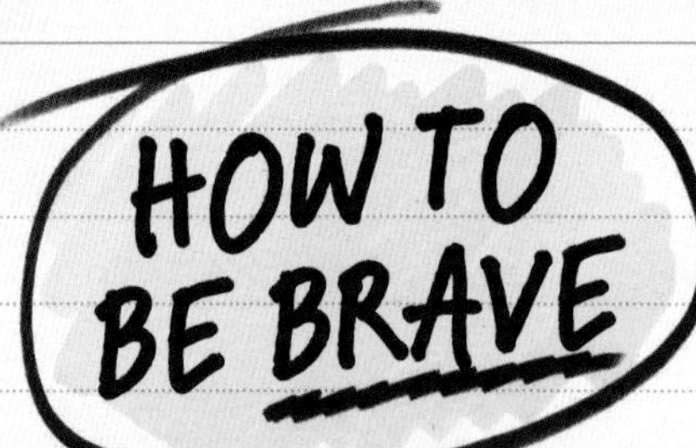

You're going to have to be brave, and I'm a teacher, so I'm going to teach you how.

Keep that chin up, even when scared. Especially when scared.

2. Find your strength. It might be drawing or singing or science. It might be looking after others or texting very fast. Whatever it is – own it and believe in yourself!

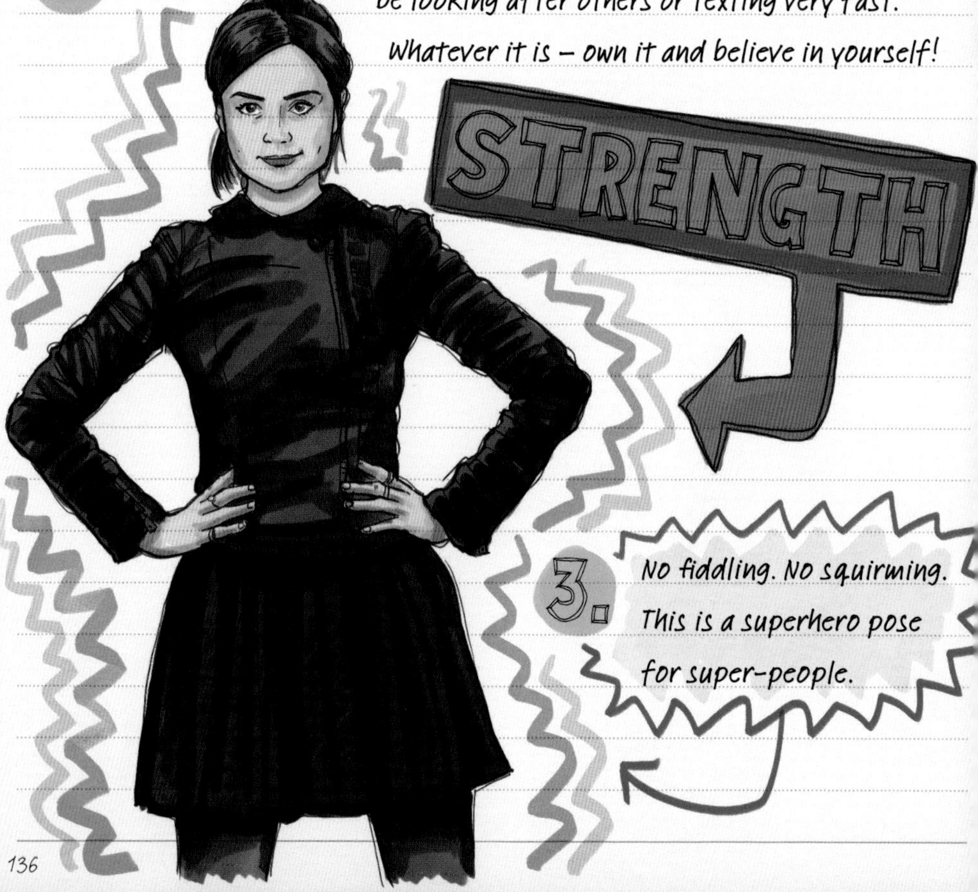

STRENGTH

3. No fiddling. No squirming. This is a superhero pose for super-people.

4. Look like a superhero, but think like the Doctor. That means think clever, think big and think about keeping everyone safe.

5. Keep eye contact at all times – not just with Weeping Angels, but all monsters.

6. Big secret here – pretending to be brave makes you feel brave. Strange but true.

PRETEND

ALL ABOUT ALIENS: THE MASTER

The Master, the Mistress, Missy . . . Whatever you call him or her, just don't forget that this terrible Time Lord is cold, cruel and calculating. Like the Doctor, the Master has regenerations and access to loads of Time Lord tech.

The Seventh Doctor and Ace faced the Master when he took control of the Cheetah People on the Cheetah World. He kidnapped Ace's friends from London! The Doctor and the Master fought, but then the Doctor decided violence wasn't the answer . . .

The Master tried to steal the Eighth Doctor's regenerations, but Grace was able to stop him. This version of the Master ended up falling into the Eye of Harmony in the TARDIS.

The Master became the Prime Minister of the UK, calling himself Harold Saxon. With hundreds of Toclafane aliens at his command, the Master captured the Doctor and turned the Earth into a giant weapons shop. Martha walked the Earth, spreading the Doctor's story and creating enough power to stop the Master.

When Davros summoned the Doctor, Missy helped us escape from the Daleks, but then she trapped me inside one of them. Luckily for me, the Doctor is clever and he saved me.

HOW TO HELP THE DOCTOR DEFEAT HIM/HER:

There's not a lot you can do to defeat the Master/Missy. The Doctor is so desperate to make the Master/Missy do the right thing – there's a bond between them. Trust the Doctor and trust yourself. Just don't trust that Time Lord!

WHERE ARE THEY NOW?

You're travelling with the Doctor now, but that doesn't mean you always will be. After the most fantastic of hellos, you'll always need to be prepared for the saddest of goodbyes.

BLASTED BACK IN TIME

AMY AND RORY

When you travel in time and space with the Doctor, two things are certain:

1. You can end up anywhere.
2. There will always be monsters and villains after you.

Amy and Rory managed to defeat a load of Weeping Angels, but one sent Rory back in time. Amy went with him. Always be on the lookout for Weeping Angels!

MEMORY WIPE

Not only did the Tenth Doctor's spare hand and spare regeneration energy create a spare Doctor, it also turned Donna into the DoctorDonna. But that was too much Time Lord knowledge for a human to take, so the Doctor had to wipe her mind. All of those thoughts and memories and adventures – gone. I would never let that happen to me!

DONNA

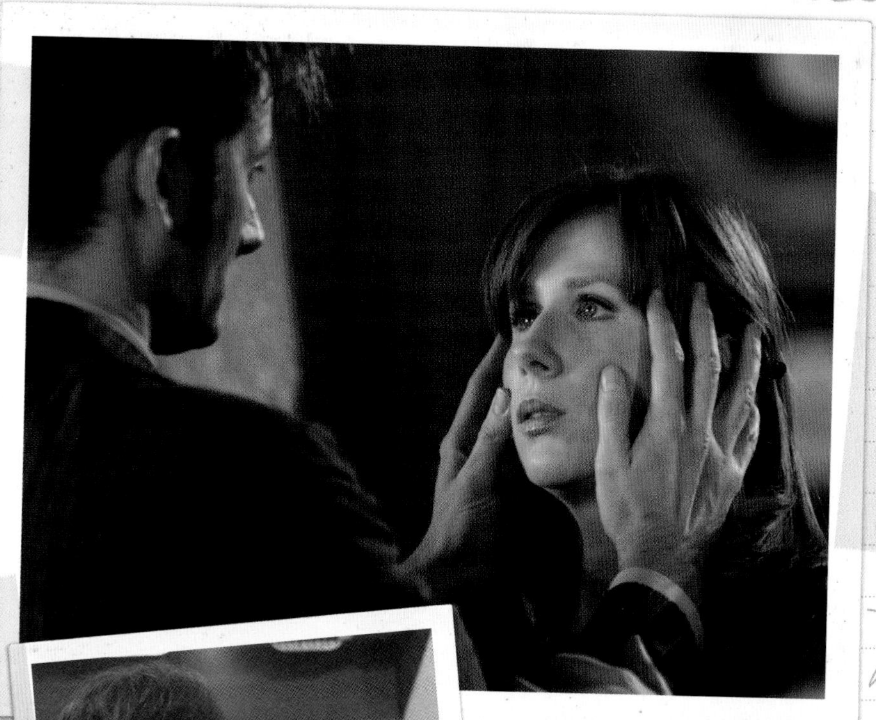

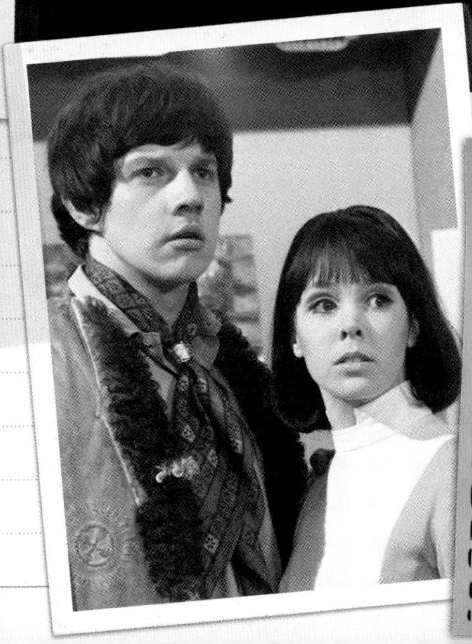

JAMIE AND ZOE

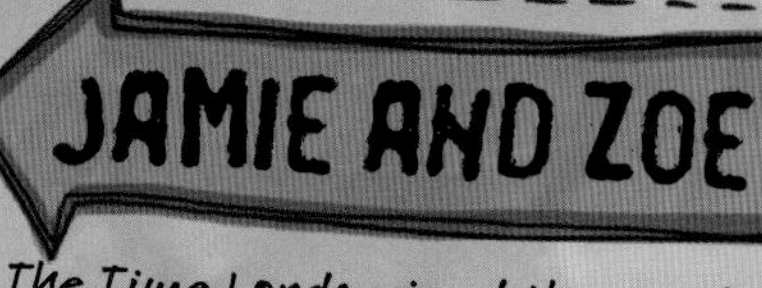

The Time Lords wiped the minds of these companions too, altering their memories. For this reason

I SERIOUSLY recommend keeping a diary.

SACRIFICE

Spending so much time with a hero makes you act like a hero yourself. There's nothing wrong with that, but heroes have to make sacrifices. River Song gave up her life to stop the Doctor giving up his, saving thousands of people trapped in the Library's Data Core. Adric sacrificed his life trying to stop the Cybermen damaging Earth. And Astrid Peth saved the Doctor from Max Capricorn on the Titanic, but didn't survive.

ASTRID PETH

PARALLEL UNIVERSE

After a huge battle with Daleks and Cybermen, Rose was trapped in a parallel universe without the Doctor. Then the walls between universes went a bit funny when the Daleks tried to destroy reality, so Rose joined the Doctor and his Children of Time in stopping Davros. The Doctor dropped Rose back in the parallel universe, but left the human Doctor with her as a present. Good present, that!

ROSE TYLER

HUMAN DOCTOR

JACKIE TYLER

STAYING BEHIND

You might just want to stop travelling with the Doctor. Enough might be enough.

Martha spent a year battling the Master, who had captured the Doctor and her family. Also, she realised she had feelings for the Doctor, and she needed to put her time into herself and her family. Other companions, such as Ian, Barbara, Victoria and Nyssa, decided their TARDIS time was up too.

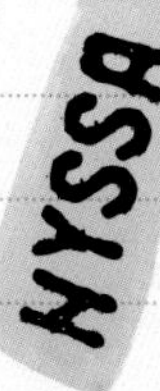

It isn't always easy bringing your new love with you in the TARDIS. (Poor Mickey, Rory and Danny really had a hard time at first!) To name a few, Vicki, Leela and Jo Grant all left the Doctor in the name of love.

JO GRANT

LEELA

LEFT WAITING

SARAH JANE SMITH

When the Doctor was summoned back to Gallifrey, Sarah Jane Smith was just dropped off. And not even where she lived! The Doctor does come back eventually, just ask Amy Pond – and Sarah Jane, actually. She travelled with the Doctor again, and had even more of her own adventures.

The Doctor's granddaughter, Susan, met a man on Earth. She wasn't sure about leaving the Doctor, but he ran off with his blue box, leaving her to be happy.

SUSAN

UNIT REPORT

'THE DOCTOR'

A personal statement by Josephine Grant

Back in those days, it was different for women. I was brought into UNIT as a civilian. The Brigadier really did only want someone to hand the Doctor test tubes and tell him how brilliant he was! I did a lot more than that: I fell under the Master's hypnotic spell and brought a bomb into UNIT HQ, for instance . . .

NOT A STATEMENT OF DEPARTMENTAL POLICY

What I didn't know about science I made up for in enthusiasm and by following my own instincts. I didn't have to pretend when telling the Doctor how brilliant he was – he really was amazing. Clever, distinguished and a real gentleman. You can see how wonderful he is, especially when compared to the Master – a Time Lord who uses his advantages for terrible things. He was always hypnotising and controlling people. I offered to sacrifice myself to save the Doctor – that's how important he is.

I've helped the Thals battle Daleks, I've assisted the Solonians and I've learned how to resist the Master's hypnosis. And life after the Doctor? I've done so much more.

Jo

My Guide to the Doctors

By River Song

Hello, sweetie! Want to know more about the Doctor? Then you've come to the right lady. I'm a child of the TARDIS – I was raised to kill him and gave up everything to save him. In between all of that, we've had some marvellous adventures.

I've met all the right Doctors in the wrong order and had to wipe their minds to make them forget. There are things I won't tell Clara, or anyone – I'm only an echo now, so every wonderful memory I have is precious.

First Doctor

There he is – the youngest Doctor. But boy, was he old! Still, he had the sense to escape Gallifrey – or Yawnsville, as I call it! Treat him kindly and listen to him.

Second Doctor

Not for me, this one. All fur coat and dancing around. He got in trouble for meddling with time, which is a little unfair if you think how much worse he's become since!

Third Doctor

Pretty classy. Guess who taught him Venusian aikido? He was a little bit tied to his job, though – working at UNIT. Be respectful and calm with this Doctor – he deserves it.

Fourth Doctor

That scarf! That hat! This Doctor was a hoot! He had a pretty loud voice, though, so I did have some earplugs in under all of this hair . . . Let him lead the way – you won't be bored!

Fifth Doctor

Look at him! This was the kind of Doctor you'd take home to meet your mother – if your mother wasn't already a companion travelling through time and space with him. He likes good tea and good manners.

Sixth Doctor

I tried to give this Doctor some fashion advice – he took all of my suggestions at once and ended up looking like this. I called him the Oncoming Rainbow. Like all Doctors, he's one of a kind.

Seventh Doctor

He could be pretty tricky, so it was hard to keep up with him. Luckily I'm me, so it wasn't too tough. Go along with his games, because if you pass his tests you'll be a better you.

Eighth Doctor

This curly-haired chap lost his memory for a bit and went on about being part human. Maybe he had a conversation with someone who was part Time Lord, who put that thought in his head? Spoilers! He might need some guidance, but as long he follows his hearts he'll be a hero.

War Doctor

This Doctor regenerated to become a soldier. He had the weight of the universe on his shoulders, so he can be forgiven for that frown. He's clever and understands the importance of life and peace.

Ninth Doctor

He was a serious man with bursts of brilliance. Or a brilliant man with bursts of seriousness. I can't quite remember, but I know that Rose Tyler made him even more brilliant. Well done, sweetie. Be patient with him and expect the unexpected.

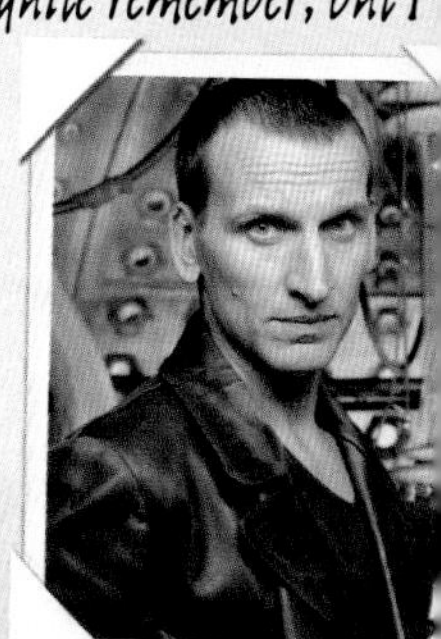

Tenth Doctor

When I called the Doctor for help in the Library I never expected to see this younger version. He was fun, wasn't he? He knew how to wear a suit, but those shoes . . . Hmm. He wasn't good at being alone, so if you ever meet him, make sure he's got someone.

Eleventh Doctor

That face! So much of it, and it's perfect in every way. He had terrible taste in hats, though, and he seemed to think the most uncool things were cool. He nearly destroyed the universe on many occasions too. But all is forgiven. You'll need energy to keep up with him and you'll need to be strict about his choice of accessories.

Twelfth Doctor

I spent twenty-four years on a date with this furious-looking thing. Amazing. Every second of it. Apart from when we had an argument and he lived with otters for a month. That man knows how to sulk in style. He needs you to listen so you can say the things he doesn't know how to say.

Thirteenth Doctor

Well, I don't think anyone saw this coming! The Doctor finally

WHO CAN HELP? PART 3:

CRAIG OWENS AND BRIAN WILLIAMS

When things seem bad, when everything is all about aliens and robots and ghosts . . . you might just need some humans to help you.

WHO IS HE?

Craig Owens is the Doctor's friend. The Eleventh Doctor was Craig's lodger for a while when he was trapped on Earth. Craig has helped the Doctor battle an alien spaceship auto-pilot and Cybermen – just by being himself. Someone who is happy where he is and in love with his family. Ahhhh. Bless.

HOW CAN HE HELP?

Okay, so he can't really fight or drive a spaceship or travel through time and he's not that clever . . . but he always has a spare room for the Doctor, and he cares about him. That's not just enough – that can be everything.

LET HIM:

- Make you a cup of tea.
- Show you how to play football.

DON'T LET HIM:

- Get into danger.
- Try to defeat every alien with love.

BRIAN WILLIAMS

WHO IS HE?

Brian Williams is Rory Williams's dad, Amy Pond's father-in-law and River Song's grandfather. He's pretty handy at playing golf and carrying out light DIY. After an adventure with the Doctor, Brian got a taste for travel and exploring!

HOW CAN HE HELP?

Need some help painting? He's your guy. Want to improve your golf swing? Speak to Brian. Want to catch up with someone who spoke to the Doctor about what happens to companions when they're lost or gone? Brian's your man.

LET HIM:

- Paint your lounge.
- Keep a (very thorough) video log.

DON'T LET HIM:

- Get sad thinking about Rory.
- Ride any more dinosaurs.

My memories are vague and I'm not allowed to keep them. I cannae remember leaving Scotland, let alone the planet. I'll draw for you what I can.

Aye, I stayed true to the Doctor.

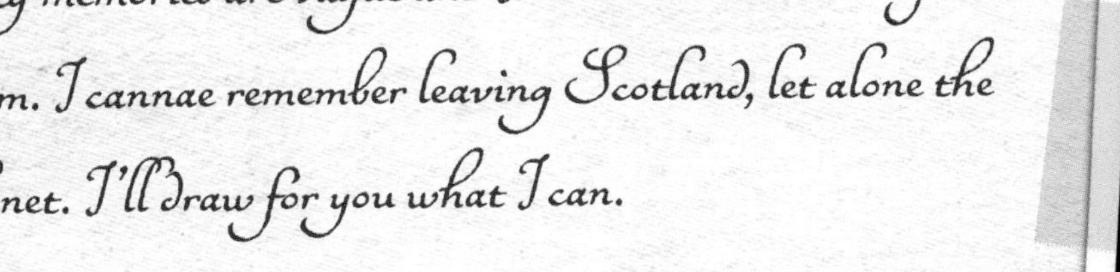

I remember a man who was clever and would lay traps of the mind for the enemies he faced. A man who was not really a man, but a lord of time who travelled throughout space in his wee blue box and treated me as his closest ally. He would joke and play the fool, but all the time he was thinking, thinking, thinking. You've never met a sharper man.

I was never the brightest, but I was always bold. Aye, I could ride a horse or scale a mountain. I even wore my kilt in Tibet. That's as bold as a man could get. I fought beasties – lots of them. Creatures from outer space who could change their faces, or metal beasties that wanted to dominate our very planet.

He wanted me to teach him how to play the bagpipes. There was talk in my clan of the Phantom Piper who would appear to a McCrimmon before death. I sometimes wondered if this could be the Doctor . . . But here I am. Aye, I wish I could keep these memories, but what would I do with them?

Jamie McCrimmon

ALL ABOUT ALIENS:

CYBERMEN

These emotionless creatures turn humans into Cybermen. If you can't be upgraded, they'll delete you.

When Cybermen and all sorts of bonkers people were trying to get hold of a living metal from Gallifrey, the Seventh Doctor played them off against one another. Ace used her slingshot to damage a Cyberman with a gold coin. I like her.

Amy Pond had a run-in with a disconnected Cyberhead which guarded the Pandorica under Stonehenge. It had a rotting old skull in it and loads of scary wires. Luckily Roman Rory turned up!

Missy turned Earth's dead into Cybermen – including my Danny. She didn't count on brave soldiers like Danny Pink and the Brigadier fighting back. They sacrificed themselves to save the world and their loved ones.

Zoe Heriot helped stop a Cyberman invasion when she used her tech skills to blow up Cyberships heading to Earth. Pretty cool, huh?

HOW TO HELP THE DOCTOR DEFEAT THEM:

Tricky, but here're a few tips. Tell them you're the Doctor and see how they feel about that. Some can't deal with gold. And Cybermen cannot handle emotions, so give them a whole heap of love and watch their heads explode.

WHO CAN HELP? PART 4:

MISSY AND ASHILDR

Okay, I know these are weird suggestions for helpful people. And I'm saying that after suggesting alien con artists and armies with guns. But if things get truly terrible then enemies can be the best of friends.

WHO IS SHE?

You know who she is and who she has been and what she's done. She's a monster, but she's also a Time Lord, and the Doctor's best friend and worst enemy rolled into one. I'm not a fan, let's just say that.

HOW CAN SHE HELP?

If the Doctor is in terrible danger and it's not because of Missy, then she'll want to know WHO is trying to cause more trouble than her. She's super clever, so she'll get you answers.

LET HER:

- Lead you to the Doctor.
- Tackle the toughest of aliens.

DON'T LET HER:

- Hurt anyone.
- Put you in a trap.

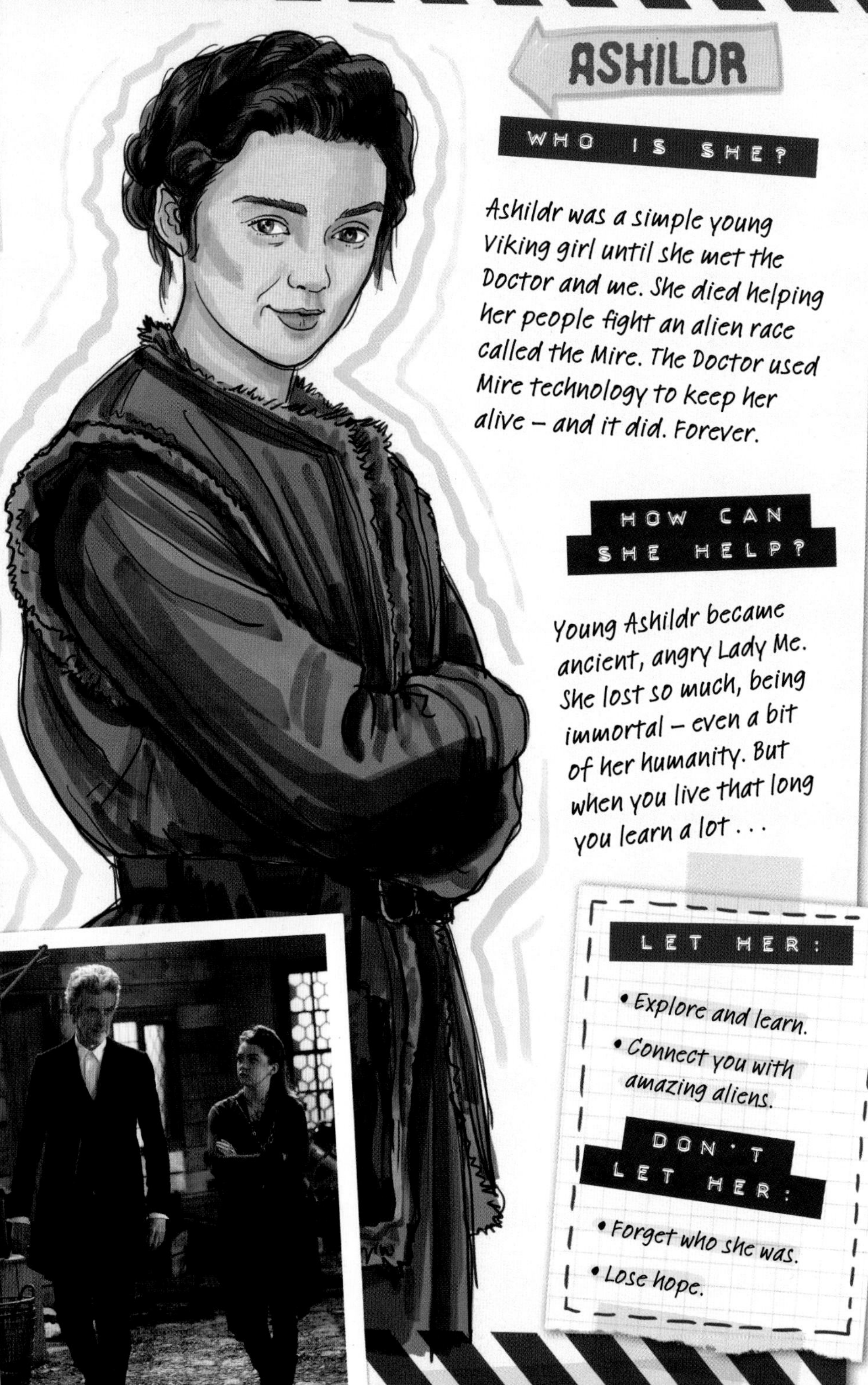

ASHILDR

WHO IS SHE?

Ashildr was a simple young Viking girl until she met the Doctor and me. She died helping her people fight an alien race called the Mire. The Doctor used Mire technology to keep her alive – and it did. Forever.

HOW CAN SHE HELP?

Young Ashildr became ancient, angry Lady Me. She lost so much, being immortal – even a bit of her humanity. But when you live that long you learn a lot . . .

LET HER:

- Explore and learn.
- Connect you with amazing aliens.

DON'T LET HER:

- Forget who she was.
- Lose hope.

Dear Grandfather,

You told me one day you shall come back, and I hold you to that. I found love and remained on Earth while you continued wandering the Fourth Dimension. I know you left me here to live a life, and I am grateful. I have the home and identity I have always wanted. But oh, the adventures we had!

You said that there must be no regrets or tears or anxieties, but how could I promise such a thing?

There have of course been all of these things, Grandfather, but I have gone forward in all my beliefs as you have advised, and I trust wholly that you are not mistaken in yours. Some find you fierce and worry that you play dangerous games. You can be difficult and stubborn. But you are truly my grandfather and have taken care of me since Gallifrey, with wisdom and love. You dared to take a Type 40 TARDIS to explore the universe . . . and I am grateful that I went with you.

Yours truly,

Susan

TARDIS TRAVEL ESSENTIALS!

Forget the bag – pack a suitcase. Donna Noble had the right idea when she moved in to the TARDIS!

PART FOUR

A PEN

Never ever leave the house without a pen. You might need to mark yourself if you see a Silent so you don't forget about it. Or you might need to write a funny poem for a sad Adipose. You might even need to keep a journal of impossible things!

Oh Sad Adipose!
How I do love thee,
small lump of lard . . .

OOD REPELLENT

We know that Natural Ood are graceful, soulful, spiritual creatures. They're not all red-eyed maniacs or pushy waiters . . . but those ones still CREEP ME OUT! It's just that they always chase you around the room with their wiggly faces, trying to make you cups of tea.

One spray of this tends to keep them away – it's made from tomato sauce. (Maybe they're scared someone will try to eat their spaghetti faces?)

PSYCHIC PAPER

Okay, so this is actually something you'll have to borrow from the Doctor, rather than bring from home. But he won't mind. Especially if he doesn't know!

IT'S EASY TO USE – HERE'S HOW:

Step 1: ~~Steal~~ Borrow Psychic Paper from the Doctor.

Step 2: Hold it and think really hard about what you want it to say.

Step 3: Whoever you show it to will see an official ID or letter or whatever you need.

Step 4: Do not leave it on the bus when visiting Aunty Joan in Birmingham.

ALL ABOUT ALIENS: SILURIANS

Lizards from the dawn of time. These guys aren't aliens – they were on Earth first – but some of them have a real problem with humans. Like, using-heat-rays-on-us type problems.

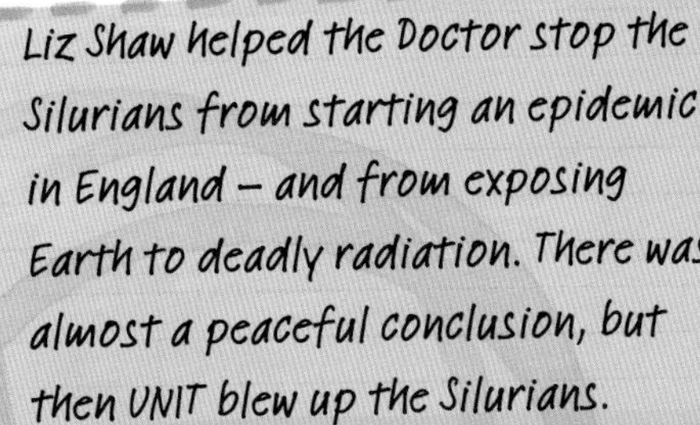

Liz Shaw helped the Doctor stop the Silurians from starting an epidemic in England – and from exposing Earth to deadly radiation. There was almost a peaceful conclusion, but then UNIT blew up the Silurians.

ny became the voice of humankind hen she was pulled underground by lurians. They'd been woken from ibernation by a human drilling roject – and they weren't very appy about it.

Poor old Rory was blasted by Restac, an angry Silurian who tried to use her heat-ray on the Doctor after a human killed her sister. She thought all humans were apes and she didn't want to negotiate with them.

Not all Silurians are bad – take Madame Vastra, for instance. She gave me a telling-off about not getting used to the Doctor's new face. She's brave, fair and clever, so she's allowed to give me a telling-off every now and again.

HOW TO HELP THE DOCTOR DEFEAT THEM:

Some want peace and some want Earth all to themselves. Talk to them and reason with them. The ones that try to blast you with heat-rays and whip you with their tongues have woken up grumpy and need help going back to sleep!

HOW TO MANAGE THE DOCTOR

Kate Stewart here, for an informal but highly confidential briefing on how to manage the Doctor. He might be a time-travelling hero, but he's still on the payroll. Here are my top tips.

TIP 1

GO FOR THE TARDIS

The TARDIS is his favourite toy. If you can't find the Doctor then find his TARDIS – just airlift it to UNIT HQ and he'll soon turn up. (N.B. We recommend you make sure the Doctor isn't inside the TARDIS first.)

TIP 2

FLATTER HIM

He loves to hear how clever he is. We all do, really. Luckily I've got Osgoods here – and if there's one thing they know how to do, it's suck up to the Doctor. He is brilliant, of course. The Osgoods are brilliant too. This is UNIT, after all – we only accept the best.

TIP 3

GIVE HIM ROOM

The Third Doctor had his own lab to play around in, and he also liked having the garage so he could tinker around with his car, Bessie.

TIP 4

REMEMBER WHO'S BOSS

Yes, he's the boss. And you'd do well to remember that. Because whatever his methods, whatever his madness, he'll do whatever it takes to save the world. He might not like being called the President of Earth, but he does suit the title.

TIP 5

GET ALL THE INFORMATION

Never stop asking questions. The more we know about the Doctor, the more we can help him. That's why we've set up the Black Archive – it's packed with artefacts, interviews, photos and stories about the Doctor. Expect your invitation soon.

CLARA'S COMPANION QUIZ

Okay, you've read my guide, but does that mean you're ready to travel with the Doctor? Take my mega-quiz to see if you've earned the companion certificate!

PART ONE: ALL ABOUT THE DOCTOR

1. WHERE IS THE DOCTOR FROM?

a) Gallifrey b) Mondas c) Karn

2. HOW MANY HEARTS HAS HE GOT?

a) Five b) Two c) One

3. WHAT IS THE NAME OF HIS SPACESHIP?

a) Bessie b) The TARDIS c) The Vortex Manipulator

4. WHAT IS HE?

a) Time Lord b) Time Master c) Space Lord

5. WHAT IS THE NAME OF HIS GRANDDAUGHTER?

a) Rose b) Barbara c) Susan

6. WHICH OF THESE SONICS HAS HE NEVER USED?

a) Screwdriver b) Pencil c) Sunglasses

7. WHO ARE HIS DEADLIEST ENEMIES?

a) Pigeons b) The Ood c) The Daleks

8. WHAT IS HIS CAR CALLED?

a) Bessie b) Martha c) Rani

9. WHAT CAN HE NOT USE HIS SONIC SCREWDRIVER ON?

a) Robots b) Gangers c) Wood

10. WHAT'S IT CALLED WHEN THE DOCTOR BECOMES SOMEONE NEW?

a) Regeneration b) Relaunching c) Reintegration

11. WHICH DOCTOR IS THIS?

a) Fifth b) Sixth c) Seventh

12. WHICH DOCTOR IS THIS?

a) Second b) First c) Twelfth

13. WHICH DOCTOR IS THIS?

a) Ninth b) Eighth c) Tenth

14. WHICH DOCTOR IS THIS?

a) War b) Second c) Seventh

15. WHICH DOCTOR IS THIS?

a) Third b) Twelfth c) Fourth

PART TWO: ALL ABOUT THE ALIENS

Name these aliens just by looking them in the eyes!

1.

a) Dalek

b) Cyberman

c) Ood

2.

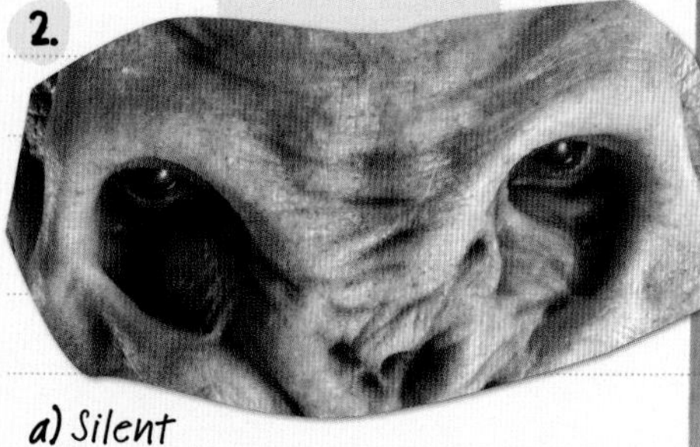

a) Silent

b) Kraal

c) Reaper

3.

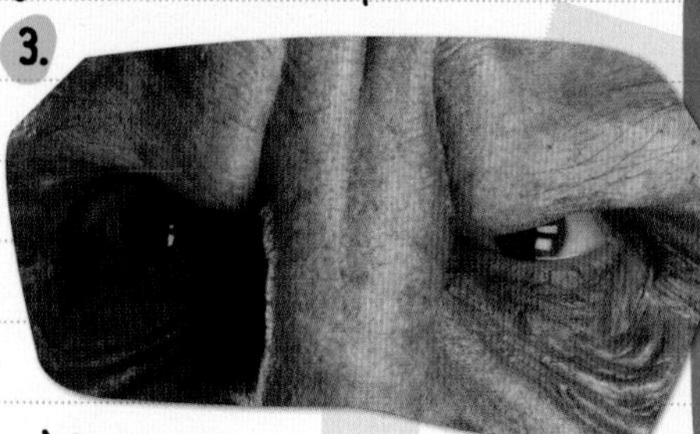

a) Sensorite

b) Sontaran

c) The Master

4.

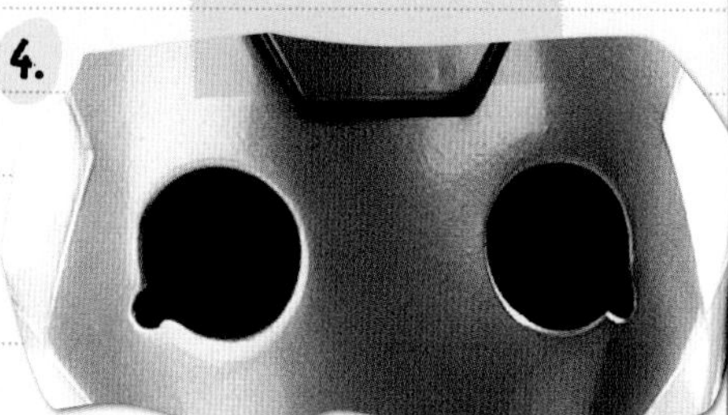

a) Boneless

b) Ganger

c) Cyberman

5.

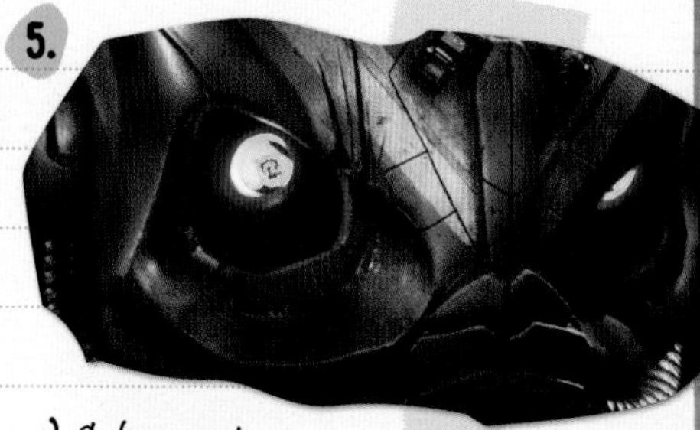

a) Cybermat

b) Skovox Blitzer

c) Gelth

6.

a) Weeping Angel

b) Sycorax

c) Hath

7.

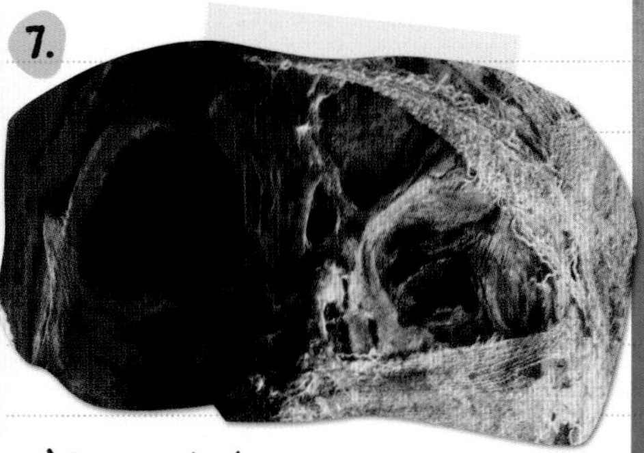

a) Dream Crab

b) Heavenly Host

c) Foretold

8.

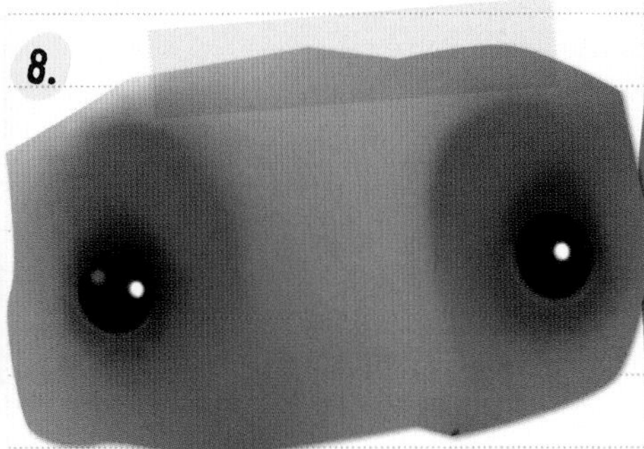

a) Werewolf

b) Adipose

c) Dalek

9.

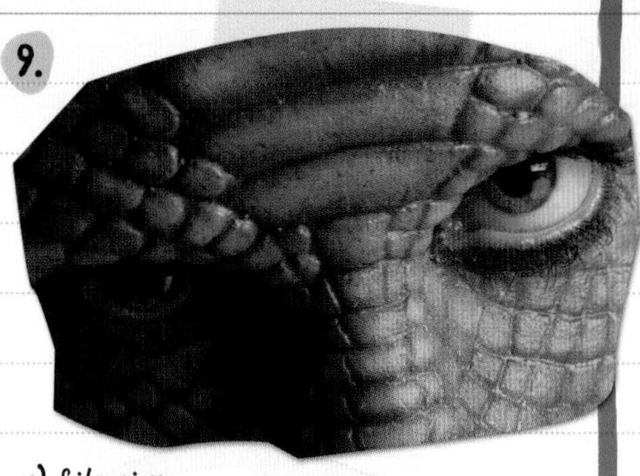

a) Silurian

b) Racnoss

c) Ganger

10.

a) Zygon

b) Thal

c) Judoon

PART THREE: ALL ABOUT THE COMPANIONS

1. WHAT IS SARAH JANE'S LAST NAME?

a) Smith b) Tyler c) Grant

2. WHERE WAS TEGAN TRYING TO GET TO WHEN SHE MET THE DOCTOR?

a) Gatwick Airport

b) Heathrow Airport c) Australia

3. WHAT WAS AMY WILLIAMS'S NAME BEFORE SHE GOT MARRIED?

a) Amy Pond b) Amy Song

c) Amy Melody

4. WHAT WAS ROSE TYLER'S MUM CALLED?

a) Francine b) Sylvia c) Jackie

5. WHERE DID THE SEVENTH DOCTOR MEET ACE?

a) Iceworld b) Mondas c) Sontar

6. WHAT IS MARTHA JONES'S JOB?

a) Nurse b) Doctor c) Vet

7. WHERE DID THE ELEVENTH DOCTOR MEET OSWIN?

a) The Dalek Asylum

b) The Dalek Factory c) Skaro

8. WHAT WAS ROSE TYLER'S BOYFRIEND CALLED?

a) Marty b) Mikey c) Mickey

9. WHERE WAS JAMIE MCCRIMMON FROM?

a) Scotland b) Ireland c) Poosh

10. WHICH OF THESE COMPANIONS DIDN'T WORK FOR UNIT?

a) Susan b) Jo Grant c) Mike Yates

ANSWERS:

PART ONE

1. a
2. b
3. b
4. a
5. c
6. b
7. c
8. a
9. c
10. a
11. a
12. b
13. c
14. c
15. b

PART TWO

1. a
2. a
3. b
4. c
5. b
6. a
7. c
8. b
9. a
10. c

PART THREE

1. a
2. b
3. a
4. c
5. a
6. b
7. a
8. c
9. a
10. a

How many did you get right?

1–10

WAIT FOR THE NEXT ADVENTURE!

You're not quite ready to be a companion. You need to take a little bit more time to learn about time and give yourself some space to learn about space.

11–29

GET IN THE BOX!

You're so ready to be a companion! I recommend you get your running shoes on now, and listen for the VWROOP VWROOP of the TARDIS!

30–35

WAIT! ARE YOU THE DOCTOR?

There's KNOWING ABOUT the Doctor and BEING the Doctor – and you might be the Doctor. Or a very clever Cyberman which has two brains squished into its head.

COMPANION CERTIFICATE

You passed my tests and you have what it takes to travel through time and space.

I, Clara Oswald, declare you ready to be

THE DOCTOR'S COMPANION

If you agree to run with the Doctor, save the universe,
battle aliens, stop him when he goes too far,
push him when he won't go far enough and
be the very best friend you can be,
then sign your name below:

....

Run, you clever thing, and remember me. C.O.x

Oh, Clara.

Clara, Clara, Clara. You can't explain me in a book! I'm the Oncoming Storm. I'm an enigma. I'm Doctor Disco. I'm . . . slightly offended, actually.

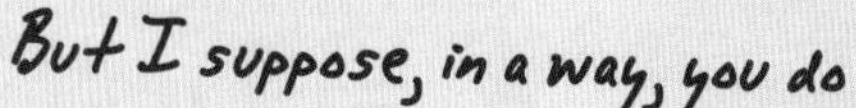

But I suppose, in a way, you do know all about me. You definitely don't know how to get around the TARDIS or what my faces really mean. But you understand me. You're bossy, and a control freak, and you're brilliant. We really do deserve each other.

All of these companions . . . their memories and their letters and their notes. Their long days and their short lives. Their journeys with me might end, but my journeys with them never will.

I'll put this back where you hid it, and I'll pretend I never saw it. I'll pretend there won't be others. But know this: I'll never forget you, my Impossible Girl.

The Doctor

P.S. Nice quizzes. I do like a quiz. So very you.